Short
Stories
Three

Compiled by Roger Mansfield

Illustrated by John Dugan

SCHOFIELD & SIMS LTD., HUDDERSFIELD

0 7217 0302 x

0 7217 0332 1 Net edition

First printed 1977

Short Stories is a series of three books:

SHORT STORIES ONE	0 7217 0300	3
SHORT STORIES TWO	0 7217 0301	1
SHORT STORIES THREE	0 7217 0302	x

Printed in England by Garnett Print, Rotherham & London

CONTENTS

ACKNOWLEDGEMENTS

The compiler and publishers wish to thank the following for permission to use copyright material:

Michael Joseph Ltd., for 'The Test' by William Mayne, from 'Voices'.

A. W. Sheppard, for 'The Ant Lion' from 'The Nature of Love' by Judith Wright.

Jack Schaefer, for 'Jacob' from 'First Blood' by Jack Schaefer, published by Andre Deutsch, for British Commonwealth rights, and Harold Matson Co. Inc. for Canadian rights (copyright 1952, 1953 by Jack Schaefer).

Liam O'Flaherty, for 'The Wild Goat's Kid' from 'The Short Stories of Liam O'Flaherty', published by Jonathan Cape Ltd.

Kurt Vonnegut Jr, for 'Harrison Bergeron' from 'The Best from Fantasy and Science Fiction – 11th Series', published by Mercury Press Inc.

Rigby Ltd. (Australia), for 'The Shell' by Colin Thiele from 'The Rim of the Morning'.

Faber and Faber Ltd., for 'Billy the Kid' from 'The Hot Gates' by William Golding.

Edna O'Brien and Jonathan Cape Ltd., for 'The Rug' from 'The Love Object' by Edna O'Brien.

INTRODUCTION

The line between stories for adults and stories for children is an imprecise one. Some critics and writers have even suggested that no distinction can be drawn between the two. In terms of intrinsic literary quality, this argument certainly holds true. There is no reason why lower standards should apply to literature intended for children; no reason why younger readers should be satisfied with hackneyed plots, stereotyped characters, unconvincing action or trivial themes. There are, however, other considerations. Any reader must be able to respond to a book.

> One does not write *for* children. One writes so that children can understand. Which means writing as clearly, vividly and truthfully as possible.
>
> Leon Garfield

If a story goes too far beyond a reader's experience or imagination, or if the style and vocabulary present tedious barriers, there will be no communication. And if this happens too often, there is a real possibility that reading, as an enjoyable and worthwhile recreation, will be discarded. It is on these grounds that teachers, librarians and parents are justified in distinguishing between literature for children and books for adults. But to exaggerate the gap can be as dangerous as to ignore it.

> One does indeed write *for* children, but there isn't really any Great Divide.
>
> John Rowe Townsend

The aim of this series is to reduce the risk that younger readers themselves will see a Great Divide where none exists, to present stories that are both accessible and, at the same time, capable of widening horizons—stories that the reader will *always* enjoy, whatever his or her age.

> A children's story which is enjoyed only by children is a bad children's book.
>
> C. S. Lewis

William Mayne

William Mayne was born in 1928, the eldest of five children of a doctor and a nurse. He was educated at the Canterbury Cathedral Choir School, which provided the setting for his third novel, *A Swarm in May*, the book that established him as a leading author for young people. It tells the story of John Owen, the youngest chorister at the school, who refuses to carry on tradition by acting as the cathedral's beekeeper, thinking he dislikes bees. But in helping the organist with his swarm, he discovers quite the opposite and also makes other exciting discoveries among the cathedral towers. Subsequent Choir School novels are *Chorister's Cake*, *Cathedral Wednesday* and *Words and Music*.

Several of his other books are set in the Yorkshire Dales, where he spent his own childhood and where he worked for a time as a schoolteacher. He has also worked for the BBC, although he has mostly been a full-time writer. Altogether he has produced more than twenty books for children, including *A Grass Rope*, *Earthfasts* and *Ravensgill*. He has also edited a number of anthologies.

Most of his stories are for older children, who are better able to appreciate the clever way he evokes places and atmosphere, as in A HAUNTED TERRACE and A PRINCE IN THE BUILDING, and his brilliant characterisation, of which THE TEST is a particularly good example. This story first appeared, in fact, in an anthology for adult readers.

William Mayne lives in the village of Thornton Rust in his beloved Yorkshire. He does all his writing and a great deal of reading in his comfortable stone cottage overlooking the Fells.

The Test

by William Mayne

I should think the secret is never panic. The secret of life, I mean. If you can keep cool while those about you are doing theirs and standing up on end, what's more you'll be a man and all that. You're pretty cool, Ozzie, said Mr. Barlow to me more than once, and I pride myself I am pretty cool most of the time, almost nonchalant. It just isn't my way to get excited.

So it doesn't worry me about this driving test thing I keep having to take, even if it isn't fair, the man knows the rules better than I do and then he has to decide. You see, he sends me off on the old bike. I said old, but it's new. I got a new one each time, just to show him quietly I was a bit more expert than the blokes coming in old Fords and that. He sends me round the houses, and then he goes and has a cup-of or something. Of course, at first I did what he said, going round the houses, but after a time or two I used to stop and have a cup-of myself, and then come back. Still I'll win him yet. It isn't him I'm writing about.

I'm on the river, like that water rat, only there isn't all the boiled ham and bottles of pop jazz. You've got to work, I don't know what I'd do without it, no money for one. I left today. You've got to keep calm in the face of advice, and I do anyway.

When I said river I meant canal. It was river I wrote, but it has these barges on and that makes it a canal. And locks and quays, says Mr. Barlow. And that engine. Mind you, I don't do the engine. You have to learn it slowly, Mr. Barlow says. He says slowly was the right word for me. I don't like to rush things, and he knows that. I haven't been there so long. I wasn't there so long, I mean.

I was on the cleansing before that. To be frank that means dustbins. One of the new trucks, it hitches its bottom in the air and shakes it all down if you put the lever forwards, and I didn't know you hadn't to pull it right back. We'd all that lot to shovel up again and load in, and I had to give in my uniform. We got a uniform on that job, and a cap. I wear my own clothes on this one. The one I had.

It's dredging now. I got up a bit soon today, I read the clock wrong, about an hour different, half-past five not half-past six, but it didn't matter with the weather just right, you've no idea perhaps if it's wet where you are now. The sky all one colour like a balloon, and sunshine, you never saw anything like it.

Mum wouldn't get out. She said I'd to wait. Well, I didn't. There were cold sausages, and that milk. She'd left the top loose and it sprinkled like a hose. I had to walk round it. Then I thought I'd get down to the river early, and I got the old Norton out. I always say old to be more friendly, but I only had it last week for this new test. They ought to sell a mule with each one, to kick it. Still, I got it done, and put my skid-lid on again. It falls off on the bumps and when I kick, but I don't like the straps, it feels as if your head is being carried by somebody else with them clasping you.

I was down at the river before six. I wished I'd stopped in bed then, because it was all misty. The weather isn't regular, you might have noticed. It gets worse in summer, more rain. This wasn't rain, only thin fog. I couldn't see the scoop.

There'd been a truck there all night, ready to start on first thing. It would save Harry waiting and having to brew up for something to do if I filled it for him. This dredger stands on the bank. I'll tell you what it does. It has caterpillar tracks, you know, the wheels inside a sort of chain and that goes round with them like laying its own ground, but it has to have ground under it as well, so I don't know why they have it. Mr. Barlow was telling me once, but I don't think he knows or he wouldn't have gone off shouting. People that don't know shout a lot, I've found. I don't shout if I don't know. I just tell them all the same. There's a cab next. It goes

round if you want it to. It has to, or it wouldn't work. Then there's the jib. That's the word for it. It's some girders sticking out from the cab, and it's like a thick fishing-rod in a way, not to look at, but what it does. There's a lot of lines go off from the end, and instead of a hook there's the scoop. That goes in the river and scoops up the mud. It drops in, and then there's a wire draws it in to the bank and lifts it up and it's full of this mud and water. You can't catch fish with it. It wasn't for that I said it was like a fishing-rod. I only said that because it sticks out over the water. It doesn't even look like one, but I said that before. It's more like half a bridge.

I was down there early. I could hardly see the scoop up in the mist, but you don't need to see, you can feel. Mr. Barlow says you can. He once felt a great fish in the water and scooped it out suddenly, and behold, it wasn't a fish at all. I forget what it was. I thought it was going to be a camel, and that's all I can think of now.

9

This dredger has a motor. It's diesel and you have to start it before it will go. I mean you don't just press a thing like a car, or kick it like the old Norton. You have to wind it. Mr. Barlow calls it the mangle, but that would be better for a steam-roller. Mr. Barlow says a steam-roller is only a kind of kettle, and I think the dredger is, too, because the water boils. It may surprise you to know that there is water in engines. I was surprised, too. It boils away, but you are all right near a river. We were near a river, so it was all right. There is no water in a motor bike, that is all.

I put the old (what I say, you know) Norton under the hedge. The exhaust pipe is getting colours in it instead of being silver like when it was in the shop. I got out the book and turned off the petrol. You have to follow the book for a bit or you don't know what to do. I turned to page four and got it up on its stand. It was all right then. I put my skid-lid on the saddle and my gloves on the tank, and there it was for the day. The only thing, Mum hadn't made me the sandwiches. She wasn't up.

I thought I would get the truck loaded before Harry came and please him. Well, I had to start the dredger. Mr. Barlow does it usually. I knew how to do it. You get it on half impression and pull out the knob until the light comes on. Then you just wind it. I got it half impressed, and I got the handle in its place, but it wouldn't turn, not it. Mr. Barlow just does it, and I thought I wasn't weak in the arm. It's just stuck, I thought, and I put it where I could get my foot on it and jumped on it. It went down all right, and then it came walloping up and I couldn't get out of the way, I was on it. I went cracko into the hedge and the handle went buzzing round and what a clatter. But it hadn't started. The whole dredger was shaking, you've no idea, and I remembered the control was locked in case the scoop ran down in the night. I got out of the hedge, what I could, but there was some shirt still there, and climbed in the cab again, and pulled the lever to N, which is Normal, where it won't do anything. I didn't know much about throttle but I put it up to half when I saw it. I thought it would help it to start. Then I got winding again. The red light was on. I don't know what it does, but you have to have it on for half impression or you can't turn it at all, Mr. Barlow says.

It wound now, but stiffish, but it was right, because there was

the engine inside breathing. This turning pumps the air in. Then she began crumping and there was that grey smoke, a puff or two. Then more puffs, and then the handle got so it was being taken from my hands, and then it did get taken, and went on by itself like it was sleep-walking, you know, it isn't human any more. It never done that for Mr. Barlow. But it didn't matter, it could stop there until next day, no reason why not. Only thing, it squeaked a bit.

I got up in the cab and put it on full impression and put out the red light. She was going then, I know. Mr. Barlow never got such a thump out of her when he started, and that's certain. I couldn't hear a thing, and that white smoke went up in the mist like a tower, a thin tower. It was knobbly. If it had been solid like rope you could have climbed it. But I wasn't worried about that, nowhere to climb to for one thing. I wanted to fill that truck with mud.

I sat in the seat. I wanted to begin like Mr. Barlow. He sets out his dinner on the shelf, the box and the thermos and then lights a cig. I hadn't got any of these, because Mum never got up that morning. And because I never had after that time in the bus, and I don't want to get cancelled and die before my life ends. Well, I couldn't do any of Mr. Barlow's things. He called it settling in, and when you get to my age, Ozzie, and quite a lot of so on and so on.

She was going like a washboard. I didn't know what the levers did. That's how it's done, levers. You pull them and push them, or both. There was several of them. I got hold of a couple to see what they did. First I pulled the one on the left. There was a noise like a bone being pulled off your head. I knew what to do then, press a pedal. It stops the noise. Well, it did it, when I got the right pedal. The thing is, you put the lever back and then it doesn't do anything until you take your foot off. It gives you time to think, which you couldn't with only one pair of hands, because of how stiff the levers are. I thought let's have a couple out, and I put one out on the right side. I was wanting the scoop going you see. I got these levers set, and lifted my leg up crafty and quick.

It was like a buckling bronco. It buckled me out of the seat, and I had to get back in it. I remember I did the same thing the first time I had a motor bike. I was stood across it, you have to to keep it up. I was hardly sat on it, and there was this thing you clutch, which is what you call it, but it isn't written there any more. I never saw it written. Well, on this bike I let it go, and next thing I knew I was still standing there and the bike was in a fit on the floor. Mum was in a fuss about that, because it made a mark on the wall, hitting it, and oil all over the carpet, but you've to practise somewhere.

When I was back in the seat of the dredger I looked to see what was happening. Nothing much, I thought at first. We were going round, it and me. At least, sometimes we were going round, and sometimes standing still, and then going back again. It was uneasy, like walking on somebody under the carpet, which I don't know if you've ever done, but it's worse for the person under and not too good for the one on top. But I didn't know what was causing it. I had to get out to look. Well, it was amazing. I mean, I was amazed, not funny amazed but peculiar amazed. The dredger was digging a hole in the ground with the caterpillar tracks. One of them was scooping out forwards and the other one backwards, going different ways, you see, and that's what made it uneasy.

It hadn't gone so far. I got up in the cab again and put my foot on the pedal which if it was for a hand would be a clutch. We stopped digging. I put one lever back, and I thought I'd put the other, but when I took my foot off the dredger started crawling about lopsided, it was like having one foot in your raincoat pocket. I don't know if it ever happened to you but it did to me. Well, I soon got it out of that, but before it would come there was a noise and it lost the starting-handle against the truck, sort of put it through the tyre. I could hear the bang, and the handle went up in the air and came down the other side of the river or canal. Well, it got rid of a squeak. The truck went lopsided, too, it couldn't help it.

I'd found out about two levers. They were the ones for backwards and forwards. I tried another. I was right first time. It was the scoop. It came down in the water like a beauty, and I let it to the bottom. Then there was another one to do to wind the rope in under, to make it scrape the bed of the river. The first one I tried put a sort of wobble on everything. The jib swung sideways, and then went all tight, and began to tip the whole thing over. I didn't want that, so I put the pedal down and stopped it. I found the right one next time. I could tell Mr. Barlow he could do the job quicker. The scoop came up like a submarine, and up in the air. Right, I put its lever back. Then I got the one that turns the dredge part not the walking part, and turned it. It went easy. I was surprised. First time over the truck, though, it hit the cab, but next time I had it lifted, and then I let the load out.

Harry always cleans the windscreen anyway, so what's a bit extra? I hadn't put much *in* the truck, though. I went down again for another load. I don't know what Mr. Barlow makes such a fuss for about skill and that. It only wants doing, like anything.

I got the second load in all right. The scoop went in just the right place and I let the load out. Well, that truck wasn't parked right. I couldn't get the scoop out again. Mr. Barlow never had difficulties like mine. It never caught for him. I couldn't lift it, because the side came off the truck and jammed it one way. I couldn't get it sideways for some reason or another. I was just worried I wasn't going to get the truck filled before seven o'clock. It wouldn't go. I thought it must just have got at an angle, and be just too wide, so I began to move those first levers again, you know, those that walked the dredger about. I wanted to walk it about and get the scoop out of the truck. It was the proper way to do it. I got reminded of the time I had a knitting-needle stuck down the telly, and we couldn't get it out until we moved the telly. Of course, it would happen all awkward and all the lights go out of a sudden just as we were fiddling. Well, I was. If you can't move the knitting-needle, move the telly. So I was moving this dredger.

One of the levers got stuck. I just wanted everything to stand still a minute. You see, I'd got all the levers working, and I haven't enough feet, I'm not a tripod or whatever they call it I've only got

one pair, do you think I come from Mars? All the same, I kept cool. You have to. I just let it ride, and it gets put right somehow.

I was thinking what to do. Don't get in a state, I always say. Just let it come, that's life. Don't panic. I was getting at the levers gradual, one at a time, finding the pedal and going well, but the bank must have been soft, or something of the sort, because you see what happened. I'm only telling you this so that you'll see it would have happened to Mr. Barlow the same or worse. I mean, he isn't adaptable like me. He has to arrange his dinner and his thermos, but I can do without. Really it was lucky I hadn't any, or I wouldn't have had.

This scoop was still fast as the top of the ketchup, you know how that is. The way to get that off is to squeeze it tighter in the back of the door. It softens the glass. Well, that was no good with the scoop, because there wasn't a door, only the cab door of the truck. I was moving the dredger, or it was moving, anyway, when it sort of went on its side a bit. That was when I thought the bank was giving, and I thought it would get right. I was being calm, but there wasn't time. The next thing I knew the water was coming nearer. The dredger was falling on its side, right off the land into the water.

I knew what to do. Jump out. I was cool, calm and collective. But I hadn't got the scoop out of the truck. I jumped, on to the bank. The dredger was hooked over so I could see under it like when the vacuum cleaner is getting emptied. The engine was still at it, and one of the tracks was going round still, flinging stuff out. Then there was a tremendous wallop and the scoop came flying out of the truck. I thought I was right by then, as it went just over my head, I could have touched it. All I got was a bit of mud. I was going to get back in the cab, but it was too late for that. All that held the dredger up by then was the scoop in the back of the truck. When that let go the dredger went, too. It fell on its side in the river, like going to sleep. There was a crack or two from the engine, and then nothing but a bit of a wave on the water. It went right under, not a bit of it showing, gently it went, tired like. I know I said that before, but it was like that. Then it was quiet. It would be, that time in the morning. Down there it was sunny now, with

16

the mist all going. It had mostly gone in half an hour. It was only half-past six now.

Well, I couldn't do anything. I went home. You would have done, too, only a few minutes. I could fetch my dinner. So I kicked off the old (just my way) Norton, put on the skid-lid, and went home. Mum was up then, ready to give me a bit of breakfast. I told her what happened. She thought I might get in trouble about it, but it might have happened to anyone. She said I had to get back in bed and not be so well that day, so I did, and then she said to change my job if this one made me feel ill, so I did.

Of course, I got up and done the test this evening, and I couldn't stop it outside the caff, so I didn't get anything whilst the man was drinking his. But never mind, eh, he said he would pass me this time, though I never got round to winning the questions he asked. I was just getting used to him, too.

Judith Wright

Judith Wright was born in 1915 near Armidale, New South Wales. She spent much of her girlhood on her parents' sheep station and, because there were no schools nearby, received her first education through the New South Wales Correspondence School. After graduating from Sydney University, she spent a year in Europe. When she returned to Australia, she worked as a stenographer, a secretary, a statistician and an agriculturalist. She now lives at Mount Tamborine in southern Queensland.

She is best known for her poetry, being recognised as Australia's leading contemporary poet, but her stories are also of outstanding quality. They are not, however, written in what many people falsely think of as a "poetic" style: there are no involved descriptions or exaggerated images. Instead, her prose is simple, direct and compelling.

"Outside the lighted window, something moved. Eyes watched, a hand went out and very quietly touched the window-bars; then after a while, a shadow moved round the house, from locked door to locked door ... "

The above extract comes from *The River and the Road*, one of her novels for young people. It is set in Australia in 1859—the time of horse-drawn coaches and gold prospecting—and tells the strange story of a man who cannot forget the dark, unjust days of his youth and returns to seek his revenge in the small township along the Great North Road to Sydney.

Two other books for young people, which are equally absorbing, are *Kings of the Dingoes* and *Range the Mountains High*.

The Nature of Love, the collection of short stories from which HOLIDAYS and THE ANT-LION are taken, is intended more for adult readers, as is her historical memoir *The Generations of Men*.

The Ant-Lion

by Judith Wright

"He can't get out; he can't get a hold of it," Morvenna cried. She thrust suddenly with the end of a twig, trying to push the ant up the shifting sand-slope of the pit. But her brother, lying opposite her, filled his cheeks with air and blew hard. The ant fell back to the pit-bottom, and in a moment the little fury of jaws burst out at it, seized it, vanished again. Only a flurry of sand in the bottom of the little pit marked for a few seconds the ant's last struggle.

The two children sat up slowly, breathing again. They looked at each other with a kind of guilt. Max's face was quite red; Morvenna's mouth was open.

"How many would he kill, I wonder?" Max said. "That's three we've given him, but they were all little ones. I'll get a meat-ant and see what he does."

"Oh no, Max, don't, don't. I don't want you to." Morvenna clenched her hands, but she could not help looking round in the grass for the meat-ant track that led to the ant-hill farther up the slope. Max went across to it, holding his twig, and bent down. Morvenna gave a scream. "If you do, Maxie, I'll kill the lion. I will, truly."

"Don't you dare," Max said. "It's the first ant-lion we've ever seen and we might never find another. I want to show it to everyone." He came back, holding his twig gingerly and turning it from end to end as the red ant rushed along it. Meat-ants could bite.

"Now I'll put it in," he said. "Look, Morv." He shook the twig hard over the little pit, but the ant was obstinate and clung. Angry,

19

intent, he finally dislodged it with a blade of grass.

Morvenna sat with her hands over her eyes. "No, I won't look," she said. "It's awful of you."

But the ant was in the pit. She peered through the crack between her fingers and saw it. It looked big and strong, frenziedly pulling down the sand of the slope in its struggle to escape. Perhaps it might get away. She took down her hands and leant forward.

In their minds the ant and its arena of battle enlarged, filled the whole world. Under the sand at the pit-bottom crouched the lion, big as a real lion, waiting for the ant to slide down a little farther. But this one was so big, bigger than the ant-lion itself. Max said, "Now we'll see some sport."

The ant was puzzled at the sand that slipped so treacherously and persistently away as it climbed. It stopped, slid, went down almost to the bottom. For a moment there was a stir in the sand there, and Morvenna jumped. The ant might have seen it, too; at any rate it gathered all its strength and made a rush at the slope. The sand slid quickly, but the ant was determined; he had almost reached the top. "Good ant, good ant," Morvenna cried; but Max pushed with his twig, and down went the ant to the bottom.

For a moment nothing happened. "It's *too* big," Max said, and his lips pursed. The two children stared down, lying on their stomachs, heads almost together. The ant hesitated, and began to struggle up against the slope.

But now the ant-lion moved. Quick, dexterous, it thrust its stumpy forelegs from the sand and began to jerk its head, heavy and tool-like. Sand flew up, hindering the big ant, setting the walls slipping down. "Ah," Max breathed. "Look at that now."

The ant slipped and slipped, staying in the one place. It was growing tired, but it was clearly in a panic; its legs worked frantically. The hot shadows of the tree above moved across and across; the cicadas filled the afternoon with their monotonous shrill. The battle swayed. Morvenna moved aside; her rib was against a knotted root of the tree; and as she moved Max gave a shout of triumph. "Oh, what happened?" She thrust him aside and peered down.

The ant-lion had seized the meat-ant by one leg. Those relentless tool-jaws hung on, like the jaws of a dingo harassing a sheep. The ant, caught at last, was putting out a desperate effort; his free legs thrashed wildly, he made a little headway, but the weight of the grub-like creature braced against him was too much, and he could find nothing to grip.

"I ought to save him," Morvenna thought. "I oughtn't to let . . . Mother would call it cruelty to animals." But she no longer wanted to put down her twig, even if Max would let her. Shamed, enraptured, she clung to the tree-root with one hand and stared down.

The ant grew weaker, slower, his struggles more spasmodic. The lion saw his chance now; he released the leg and made for the ant's body, seizing him by the abdomen. There was a wild scurry in the pit now, the ant rearing in the fountaining sand. They could see those shovel-jaws working.

The silence was the strangest thing, Morvenna thought. Round them the afternoon continued; a wagtail hopped on the fence, other ants ran placidly about their business, the creek below made its endless liquid noise over the rocks; but to the two children all had shrunk to the dimensions of the pit, and the creatures in it, engaged in their soundless struggle, plunged and reared enormous. The golden air should have been full of their shrieks and groanings.

Now the ant fell. All was over; his waist almost severed, his legs quivering in the air, he lay helpless. How quickly, how ruthlessly, the ant-lion pulled him down, avoiding the last kicks of those thin useless legs, touching him, severing abdomen from body, hiding him in the sand to serve for larder, where the other ants lay. The creature seemed like a little machine, a tool for some energy that possessed him; hideous, swift, he sent a shudder through Morvenna as she watched him.

Slowly, slowly the lion and his victim sank into the sand. Now they were only humps, sand-covered; now they had vanished. There lay the pit, still and innocent, its contours unchanged.

Max sat up slowly. His eyes looked large and dark.

"Are you going to put in another?" Morvenna asked. She half-hoped, half-feared it.

"No," Max said. He stood up, not looking at the pit or at Morvenna. "Enough's enough."

"Are you going to bring Harry down and show it to him?" Morvenna persisted.

"Oh, shut up," said Max. He stood uncertainly for a moment, detaching himself from the scene, from the afternoon, from Morvenna. Then he set off down the creek-bank, running faster and faster. Morvenna stood hesitating; then she, too, began to run. At last they stopped, far from the pit, exhausted and panting.

"What shall we do now?" Morvenna said.

Jack Schaefer

Jack Schaefer was born in 1907 in Cleveland, Ohio. After completing his studies at Columbia University, he worked for United Press for a year before taking up a post as assistant director of education at Connecticut State Reformatory. He resumed full-time journalism in 1939, becoming a freelance writer ten years later with the publication of his first novel, *Shane*. This book and the film which was made in 1953 are now both considered classics of the western genre. The story is simple and familiar.

A mysterious stranger, Shane, comes to live and work with the Starrets on their farm. Against his wishes he becomes involved in their struggle against Fletcher and the other cattlemen, who want to drive the farmers off the grasslands. The feud worsens until at last Fletcher calls in a professional killer. This step forces Shane to revert to his former role of gunfighter. What distinguishes the story from the majority of other westerns is its sympathetic treatment of "good" and "bad" characters and its delicate handling of personal relationships.

The same sensitivity is to be found in Jack Schaefer's other novels and short stories. These include *First Blood*, from which JACOB is taken, *The Canyon*, *Company of Cowards*, *The Kean Land* and *Old Ramon*. The title of the last book refers to an old shepherd who is put in charge of his patron's small son for a season with the sheep. As his father and grandfather have before him, the boy watches and learns from Old Ramon—about sheep, rattlesnakes, sandstorms, coyotes, wolves, loneliness and death. This theme, the sometimes painful transition from boyhood to manhood, is common to much of Jack Schaefer's work.

24

Jacob

by Jack Schaefer

Those moccasins? Mine. Though I never wore them. Had them on just once to see if they fitted. They did. A bit tight but I could get them on.

Don't touch them. The leather's old and dry and the stitching rotted. Ought to be. They've been hanging there a long time. Look close and you can see the craftsmanship. The best. They're Nez Percé moccasins. Notice the design worked into the leather. It's faint now but you can make it out. Don't know how they did that but the Nez Percé could really work leather. A professor who studied such things told me once that design means they're for a chief. For his ceremonial appearances, sort of his dress-up footwear. Said only a chief could use that design. But it's there. Right there on those moccasins.

Yes. They're small. Boy size. That's because I was a boy then. But they're a chief's moccasins all the same. Kept them down the years because I'm proud of them. And because they mind me of a man. He had a red skin. Copper would be closer the colour. A muddy copper. And I only saw him once. But he was a man.

That was a long way from here. A long way. In years and in miles. I was ten then, maybe eleven, maybe twelve, in that neighbourhood, I disremember exactly. Best I can do is place it in the late seventies. Funny how definite things like dates and places slip away and other stray things, like the way you felt at certain times and how your first wild strawberries tasted, can remain clear and sharp in your mind. We were living, my folks and my older brother and myself, in a little town in eastern Montana. Not much of a place. Just a small settlement on the railroad that wouldn't have amounted to anything except that it had a stretch of double track where a train going one direction could pull off to let one going the other get past. My father was a switchman. Looked after track and handled the west-end switch. That was why we were there.

The Indian smell was still in the air in those days. People around here and nowadays wouldn't know what that means. It was a knowing and a remembering that not so far away were still real live free-footed fighting Indians that might take to raiding again. They were pegged on treaty lands and supposed to stay there. But they were always hot over one thing or another, settlers gnawing into their hunting grounds or agents pinching their rations or maybe the government forgetting to keep up treaty payments. You never knew when they might get to figuring they'd been pushed far enough and would start council fires up in the hills and come sudden and silent out of the back trails, making trouble. It was only a year or two since the Custer affair on the Little Big Horn south-west of where we were. No one with any experience in those things expected the treaty that ended that business to hold long.

Don't take me wrong. We didn't look for Indians behind bushes and sit around shivering at night worrying about attacks. The nearest reservation was a fair jump away and if trouble started we'd know about it long before it reached us, if it ever did. Matter of fact it never did. I grew up in that territory and never once was mixed in any Indian trouble past an argument over the price of a blanket. Never even saw any fighting Indians except this once I'm telling about and then they weren't fighting any more. It was just a smell in the air, the notion there might be trouble any time. Indians were quite a topic when I was a boy and the talk of an evening chewed it plenty.

Expect I heard as much of it as any of the boys around our settlement. Maybe more. My father had been in the midst of the Sioux outbreak in Minnesota in the early sixties. He'd seen things that could harden a man. They settled his mind on the subject. "Only good Indian," he'd say, "is a dead one." Yes. That's not just a saying out of the storybooks. There were men who really said it. And believed it. My father was one. Said it and believed it and said it so often I'd not be stretching the truth past shape to figure he averaged it couple times a week and so naturally we boys believed it, too, hearing it all the time. I'll not argue with anyone wants to believe it even today. I'm only telling you what happened to me.

Hearing that kind of talk we boys around the settlement had our idea what Indians were like. I can speak for myself anyway. The Indians I saw sometimes passing through on a train or loafing around a town the few times I was in one with the folks didn't count. They were tame ones. They were scrawny mostly and they hung around where white people were and traded some and begged liquor when they couldn't buy it. They weren't dangerous or even interesting. They didn't matter more'n mules or dogs or anything like that cluttering the landscape. It was the wild ones filled my mind, the fighting kind that lived the way they always had and went on the war-path, and made the government send out troops and sign treaties with them. Can't recall exactly what I thought they looked like, but they were big and fierce and dangerous and they liked to burn out homesteaders' cabins and tie people to wagon wheels and roast them alive over slow fires, and it took a brave man to go hunting them and look at them down the sights of his gun. Days I felt full of ginger I'd plan to grow up quick and be an Indian fighter. Late afternoon, before evening chores, I'd scout the countryside with the stick I used for a gun and when I'd spot a spray of red sumac poking out of a brush clump, I'd belly-it in the grass and creep to good cover and poke my gun through and draw my bead. I'd pull on the twig knob that was my trigger and watch careful, and sometimes I'd have to fire again and then I'd sit up and cut another notch on the stick. I had my private name for that. Making good Indians, I called it.

What's that got to do with those moccasins? Not much I guess. But I'm telling this my way. It's all part of what I remember when I sit back and study those moccasins a spell.

The year I'm talking about was a quiet one with the Sioux but there was some Indian trouble all right, along in the fall and a ways away, over in the Nez Percé country in Idaho. It started simple enough like those things often did. There was this band lived in a valley, maybe seven hundred of them all told, counting the squaws and young ones. Biggest safe estimate I heard was three hundred braves, fighting men I mean. Can't remember the name of the valley, though I should. My brother settled there. But I can recall the name of the chief. That sticks. Always will. Not the Indian of it because that was a fancy mouthful. What it meant. Mountain Elk. Not that exactly. Big-Deer-That-Walks-the-High-Places. Mountain Elk is close enough. But people didn't call him that. Most Indians had a short name got tagged to them somehow and were called by it. His was Jacob. Sounded funny first time I heard it but not after I'd been hearing it a while.

As I say, this trouble started simple enough. We heard about it from the telegraph operator at the settlement who took his meals at our place. He picked up information relaying stuff through his key. News of all kinds and even military reports. Seems settlers began closing in around Jacob's valley and right soon began looking at the land there. Had water which was important in that country. Some of them pushed in and Jacob and his boys pushed them back out. So complaints were being made and more people wanted to move in, and talk went around that land like that was too good for Indians anyway because they didn't use it right, the way white men would, and when there was enough steam up a government man went in to see Jacob. Suggested the band would be better off living on some outside reservation. Get regular rations and have an agent to look after them. No, Jacob said, he and his were doing all right. Had been for quite a spell and expected to keep on doing the same. Sent his thanks to the Great White Chief for thinking about him but he wasn't needing any help. So after a while the pressure was stronger and another government man went in. Offered to buy the land and move the band in style to a reservation. No, said Jacob, he and his children—he called them all his children though he wasn't much past thirty himself—he and his children liked their land and weren't interested in selling. Their fathers had given up land too much in the past and been forced to keep wandering and had found this place when no one wanted it, and it was good and they had stayed there. Most of them then living had been born there and they wanted to die there, too, and that was that.

Well, the pressure went on building and there were ruckuses here and yonder around the valley when some more settlers tried moving in and a bunch of young braves got out of hand and killed a few. So another government man went in, this time with a soldier escort. He didn't bother with arguing or bargaining. He told Jacob the Great White Chief had issued a decree and this was that the whole tribe was to be moved by such and such a date. If they went peaceable, transportation would be provided and good rations. If they kept on being stubborn, soldiers would come and make them move and that would be a bad business all around. Yes, said Jacob, that would be a bad business but it wouldn't be his doing. He and his children wouldn't have made the storm but they would stand up to it if it came. He had spoken and that was that.

So the days went along towards the date set which was in the fall I'm telling about. Jacob and his band hadn't made any preparations for leaving and the officer in charge of this whole operation thought Jacob was bluffing and he'd just call that bluff. He sent about four hundred soldiers under some colonel into the valley the week before the moving was supposed to happen, and Jacob and the others, the whole lot of them, just faded away from their village and off into the mountains behind the valley. The colonel sent scouting parties after them but couldn't make contact. He didn't know what to do in that situation so he set up camp there in the valley to wait and got real peeved when some of Jacob's Nez Percés slipped down out of the mountains one night and stampeded his stock. Finally he had his new orders and on the supposed moving day he carried them out. He put his men to destroying the village and they wiped it level to the ground, and the next morning early there was sharp fighting along his upper picket lines and he lost quite a few men before he could jump his troops into the field in decent force.

That was the beginning. The government wanted to open the valley for homesteading but couldn't without taking care of Jacob first. This colonel tried. He chased Jacob and his band into the mountains and thought overtaking them would be easy with the squaws and young ones slowing Jacob down, but Jacob had hidden them off somewhere and was travelling light with his braves. He led this colonel a fast run through rough country and caught him off watch a few times and whittled away at his troops every odd chance till this colonel had to turn back, not being outfitted for a real campaign. When he, that'd be this colonel, got back he found Jacob had beat him there and made things mighty unpleasant for those left holding the camp before slipping away again. About this time the government realised what it was up against and recalled the colonel and maybe whoever was his boss, and assigned a general—a brigadier—to the job and began mounting a real expedition.

We heard plenty about what happened after that, not just from the telegraph operator but from my brother who was busting the seams of his breeches those days and wanting to strike out for himself, and signed with the freighting company that got the contract carting supplies for the troops. He didn't see any of the fighting but he was close to it several times and he wrote home what was happening. Once a week he'd promised to write and did pretty well at it. He'd send his letters along to be posted whenever any of the wagons were heading back, and my mother would read them out to my father and me when they arrived. Remember best the fat one came after he reached the first camp and saw Jacob's valley. Took him two chunks of paper both sides to tell about it. Couldn't say enough about the thick green grass and the stream tumbling into a small lake and running quiet out again, and the good trees stepping up the far slopes and the mountains climbing on to the end of time all around. Made a man want to put his feet down firm on the ground and look out steady like the standing trees and stretch tall. Expect that's why my brother quit his job soon as the trouble was over and drove his own stakes there.

Yes. I know. I'm still a long way from those moccasins. I'm over in Idaho in Jacob's valley. But I get to remembering and then I get to forgetting maybe you're not interested in all the sidelines of what I started to tell you. I'll try to move it faster.

As I was saying, the government outfitted a real expedition to go after Jacob. A brigadier general and something like a thousand men. There's no point telling all that happened except that this expedition didn't accomplish much more than that first colonel and his men did. They chased Jacob farther and almost penned him a few times and killed a lot of braves and got wind of where his women and their kids were hidden, and forced him to move them farther into the mountains with them getting out just in time, not being able to carry much with them. But that wasn't catching Jacob and stopping him and his braves from carrying on their hop-skip-and-jump war against all whites in general and these troops in particular. Then a second general went in and about a thousand more soldiers with them and they had hard fighting off and on over a couple hundred miles and more, and the days drove on into deep winter and Jacob was licked. Not by the government and its soldiers and their guns. By the winter. He and his braves, what was left of them, had kept two generals and up to two thousand troops busy for four months fighting through parts of three states and then the winter licked him. He came to the second general under truce in what remained of his Chief's rig and took off his head-dress and laid it on the ground and spoke. His children were scattered in the mountains, he said, and the cold bit sharp and they had few blankets and no food. Several of the small ones had been found frozen to death. From the moment the sun passed overhead that day he would fight no more. If he was given time to search for his children and bring them together he would lead them wherever the Great White Chief wished.

There. I'm closer to those moccasins now even though I'm still way over in Idaho. No. Think it was in western Montana where Jacob surrendered to that second general. Well, the government decided to ship these Nez Percés to the Dump, which was what people called the Indian Territory where they chucked all the tribes whose lands weren't just cut down but were taken away altogether. That meant Jacob and his children, all that was left of them, about three hundred counting the squaws and kids, would be loaded on a special train and sent along the railroad that ran through our settlement. These Nez Percé Indians would be passing within a stone's throw of our house and we would have a chance to see them at least through the windows and maybe, if there was need for switching, the train would stop and we would have a good look.

Wonder if you can scratch up any real notion what that meant to us boys around the settlement. To me maybe most of all. These weren't tame Indians. These were wild ones. Fighting Indians. About the fightingest Indians on record. Sure, the Sioux wiped out Custer. But there were a lot more Sioux than soldiers in that scuffle. These Nez Percés had held their own mighty well against a big chunk of the whole United States Army of those days. They were so outnumbered it had got past being even a joke. Any way you figured, it had been about one brave to six or seven soldiers and those braves hadn't been well armed at the start and had to pick up guns and ammunition as they went along from soldiers they killed. Some of them were still using arrows at the finish. I'm not being funny when I tell you they kept getting bigger and fiercer in my mind all the time I was hearing about that long running fight in the mountains. It was notches for Nez Percés I was cutting on my stick now and the way I felt about them, even doing that took nerve.

The day came the train was to pass through, some time late afternoon was the first report, and all of us settlement boys stayed near the telegraph shack waiting. It was cold, though there wasn't much snow around. We'd sneaked into the shack where there was a stove, till the operator was peeved at our chattering and shooed us out, and I expect I did more than my share of the chattering because in a way these were my Indians because my brother was connected with the expedition that caught them. Don't think the other boys liked how I strutted about that. Well, anyway, the sun went down and we all had to scatter home for supper and the train hadn't come. Afterwards some of us slipped back to the shack and waited some more while the operator cussed at having to stick around waiting for word, and one by one we were yanked away when our fathers came looking for us, and still the train hadn't come.

It was some time past midnight and I'd finally got to sleep when I popped up in bed at a hammering on the door. I looked into the kitchen. Father was there in his nightshirt opening the outside door and the operator was on the step cussing some more that he'd had word the train was coming, would get there in half an hour, and they'd have to switch it and hold it till the westbound night freight went past. Father added his own cussing and pulled on his pants and boots and heavy jacket and lit his lantern. By time he'd done that I had my things on, too. My mother was up then and objecting, but my father thought some and shushed her. "Fool kid," he said, "excited about Indians all the time. Do him good to see what thieving smelly things they are." So I went with him. The late moon was up and we could see our way easy and I stayed in the shack with the operator and my father went off to set his signal and tend his switch. Certain enough, in about twenty minutes the train came along and swung on to the second line of track and stopped.

The telegraph operator stepped out and started talking to a brakeman. I was scared stiff. I stood in the shack doorway and looked at the train and I was shaking inside like I had some kind of fever. It wasn't much of a train. Just an engine and little fuel car and four old coaches. No caboose. Most trains had cabooses in those days because they carried a lot of brakemen. Had to have them to wrangle the hand brakes. Expect the brakeman the operator was talking to was the only one this train had. Expect that was why it was so late. I mean the railroad wasn't wasting any good equipment and any extra men on this train, and it was being shoved along slow when and as how between other trains.

I stood there shaking inside and the engine was wheezing some and the engineer and fireman were moving slow and tired around it, fussing with an oilcan and a tin of grease. That was the only sign of life I could see along the whole train. What light there was in the coaches, only one lantern lit in each, wasn't any stronger than the moonlight outside and that made the windows blank-like and I couldn't see through them. Except for the wheezing engine, that train was a tired and sleeping or dead thing on the track. Then I saw someone step down from the first coach and stretch and move into the moonlight. He was a soldier, a captain, and he looked tired and sleepy and disgusted with himself and the whole world. He pulled a cigar from a pocket and leaned against the side of the coach, lighting the cigar and blowing out smoke in a slow puff. Seeing him so lazy and casual, I stopped shaking and moved into the open and closer to the coach and shifted around trying to find an angle that would stop the light reflection on the windows and let me see in. Then I stopped still. The captain was looking at me. "Jee-sus," he said. "Why does everybody want to gawk at them? Even kids." He took a long drag on his cigar and blew a pair of fat smoke rings. "You must want to bad," he said. "Up so late. Go on in take a look." I stared at him, scared now two ways. I was scared to go in where those Indians were and scared not to, after he'd said I could and just about ordered I should. "Go ahead," he said. "They don't eat boys. Only girls. Only at lunchtime." And sudden I knew he was just making a tired joke, and it would be all right and I went up the steps to the front platform and peered in.

Indians. Fighting Indians. The fighting Nez Percés who had led United States soldiers a bloody chase through the mountains of three states. The big and fierce redmen who had fought many times their own number of better armed soldiers to a frequent standstill in the high passes. And they weren't big and they weren't fierce at all. They were huddled figures on the coach seats, two to a seat down the twin rows, braves and squaws and young ones alike, all dusty and tired and hunched together at the shoulders in drowsy silence or sprawled apart over the window sills and seat arms in sleep. In the dim light they looked exactly like the tame Indians I'd seen, and they seemed to shrink and shrivel even more as I looked at them and there was no room in me for any emotion but disappointment, and when I noticed the soldiers sleeping in the first seats close to me I sniffed to myself at the silly notion any guards might be needed on that train. There wasn't the slightest hint of danger anywhere around. Being on that train was no different from being off it except that it was being on a stopped train and not being outside on the ground. It didn't even take any particular nerve to do what I did when I started walking down the aisle.

The only way I know to describe it is that I was in a sort of trance of disappointment and I wanted to see everything and I went straight down the aisle looking all around me. And those Indians acted like I wasn't there at all. Those that were awake. Each of them had his eyes fixed somewhere, maybe out a window or at the floor or just at some point ahead, and didn't move them. They knew I was there. I could tell that. A feeling. A little crawling on my skin. But they wouldn't look at me. They were somehow off away in a place all their own and they weren't going to let me come near getting in there with them or let me know they even saw me outside of it. Except one. He was a young one, a boy like me only a couple years younger, and he was scrooged down against a sleeping brave—maybe his father—and his small eyes, solid black in the dim light, looked at me, and his head turned slow to keep them on me as I went past and I could sense them on me as I went on till the back of the seat shut them off.

Still in that funny trance I went into the next coach and through it and to the third coach and on to the last. Each was the same.

36

Soldiers slumped in sleep, and the huddled figures of the Indians in different pairings and sprawled positions but the effect the same and then at the end of the last car I saw him. He had a seat to himself and the head-dress with its red-tipped feathers hung from the rack above the seat. He was asleep with an arm along the window sill, his head resting on it. I stopped and stared at him and the low light from the lantern near the end of the coach shone on the coppery texture of his face and the bare skin of his chest where it showed through the fallen-apart folds of the blanket wrapped around him. I stared at him and I felt cheated and empty inside. Even Jacob wasn't big or fierce. He wasn't as big as my father. He was short. Maybe broad and rather thick in the body but not much, even that way. And his face was quiet and—well, the only word I can ever think of is peaceful. I stared at him and then I started a little because he wasn't sleeping. One eyelid had twitched a bit. All at once I knew he was just pretending. He was pretending to be asleep so he wouldn't have to be so aware of the stares of anyone coming aboard to gawk at him. And sudden I felt ashamed and I hurried to the back platform to leave the train, and in the shadow there I stumbled over a sleeping soldier and heard him rousing himself as I scrambled down the steps.

That started what happened afterwards. Expect I'm really to blame for it all. Mean to say it probably wouldn't have happened if I hadn't been hurrying and wakened that soldier. He didn't know I was there. He was too full of sleep at first and didn't know what had awakened him. While I stayed in the dark shadow by the coach, afraid to go out into the moonlight, he stood up and stretched and came down the steps without noticing me and went around the end of the train towards the wider shadow on the other side, and as he went I saw him pulling a bottle out of a pocket. I felt safe again and started away and turned to look back, and the light was just right for me to see some movement inside through the window by the last seat. Jacob was standing up. All kinds of wild notions poured through my mind and I couldn't move and then he was emerging through the rear door on to the platform and I wasn't exactly scared because I wasn't conscious of feeling anything at all except that I couldn't move. Time seemed to hang there motionless around me. Then I realised he wasn't doing anything and wasn't going to do anything. He wasn't even aware of me or if he was I was without meaning for him and he had seen me and dismissed me. He was standing quiet by the rear railing and his blanket was left inside and the cold night air was blowing against his bare chest above his leather breeches but he didn't appear to notice that. He was looking back along the double iron line of the track towards the tiny point of light that was my father's lantern by the west switch. He stood there, still and quiet, and I stayed where I was and watched him and he did not move and stood there looking far along the westward track and that was what we were doing, Jacob and I, when the soldier came back around the end of the train.

Thinking about it later I couldn't blame that soldier too much. Maybe he had orders to keep the Indians in their seats or not let them on the rear platform or something like that. Probably was worried about drinking on duty and not wanting to be caught letting anything slip with the tang plain on his breath. Could be, too, he'd taken on more than he could handle right. Anyway he was surprised and mad when he saw Jacob standing there. He reached first and pulled some object off the platform floor and when he had it I could see it was his rifle. Then he jumped up the steps and started prodding Jacob with the rifle barrel towards the door. Jacob looked at him once and away and turned slow and started to move and the soldier must have thought Jacob moved too slow because he swung the gun around to use the stock end like a club and smack Jacob on the back. I couldn't see exactly what happened then because the scuffle was too sudden and quick but there was a blur of movement and the soldier came tumbling off the platform to the ground near me and the gun landed beside him. He was so mad he tripped all over himself getting to his feet and scrabbling for the gun and he whipped it up and hip-aimed it at Jacob and tried to fire it and the breech mechanism jammed some way and he clawed at it to make it work.

And Jacob stood there on the platform, still and quiet again, looking down at the soldier with bare breast broadside to the gun. I could see his eyes bright and black in the moonlight and the shining on the coppery firmness of his face and he did not move and of a sudden I realised he was waiting. He was waiting for the

38

bullet. He was expecting it and waiting for it and he would not move. And I jumped forward and grabbed the rifle barrel and pulled hard on it. "No," I shouted. "Not like that." And the soldier stumbled and fell against me and both of us went down and someone was yelling at us and when I managed to get to my feet I saw it was the captain and the soldier was up, too, standing stiff and awkward at attention. "Damned Indian," the soldier said. "Trying to get away." The captain looked up and saw Jacob standing there and jerked a bit with recognising who it was. "He was not," I said. "He was just standing there." The captain looked at the soldier and shook his head slow. "Jee-sus," he said. "You'd have shot that one." The captain shook his head again like he was disgusted and tired of everything and maybe even of living. "What's the use," he said. He flipped a thumb at the soldier. "Pick up your gun and get on forward." The soldier hurried off and the captain looked at Jacob, and Jacob looked down at him, still and quiet and not moving a muscle. "There's fools of every colour," the captain said and Jacob's eyes brightened a little as if he understood and I expect he did because I'd heard he could speak English when he wanted to. The captain wiped a hand across his face. "Stand on that damned platform as long as you want," he said. He remembered he had a cigar in his other hand and looked at it and it was out and he threw it on the ground and swung around and went towards the front of the train again, and I wanted to follow him but I couldn't because now Jacob was looking at me.

He looked down at me what seemed a long time and then he motioned at me and I could tell he wanted me to step out further into the moonlight. I did and he leaned forward to peer at me. He reached a hand out towards me, palm flat and down, and said something in his own language and for a moment I was there with him in the world that was different and beyond my own everyday world and then he swung away and stepped to stand by the rear railing again and I knew I was outside again, outside of his mind and put away and no more to him than any other object around. He was alone there looking far down the track and it sank slow and deep in me that he was looking far past the tiny light point of my father's lantern, far on where the lone track ran straight along the slow-rising reaches of distance into the horizon that led past

41

the longest vision at last to the great climbing mountains. He was looking back along the iron trail that was taking him and his children away from a valley that would make a man want to put his feet firm on the earth and stretch tall and was taking them to an unknown place where they would not be themselves any longer but only some among many of many tribes and tongues and all dependent on the bounty of a forgetful government. It wasn't an Indian I was seeing there any more. It was a man. It wasn't Jacob, the tamed chief that even foolish kids could gawk at. It was Mountain Elk, the Big-Deer-That-Walks-the-High-Places and he was big, really big, and he was one meant to walk the high places.

He stood there looking down the track and the westbound night freight came rumbling out of the east and strained past, and he stood there watching it go westward along the track and his train began to move, creeping eastward slow and feeling forward, and I watched it go and long as I could see him he was standing there, still and quiet, looking straight out along the back trail.

Well. I've taken you to where I was headed. It's only a hop now to those moccasins. I tried to tell the other boys about it the next day and likely boasted and strutted in the telling and they wouldn't believe me. Oh, they'd believe I saw the Indians all right. Had to. The telegraph operator backed my saying I was there. Even that I went aboard. But they wouldn't believe the rest. And because they wouldn't believe me I had to keep pounding it at them, telling it over and over. Expect I was getting to be mighty unpopular. But Jacob saved me even though I never saw him again. There was a day a bunch of us boys were playing some game or other back of the telegraph shack and sudden we realised someone had come up from somewhere and was watching us. An Indian. Seemed to be just an ordinary everyday sort of tame Indian. But he was looking us over intent and careful and he picked me and came straight to me. He put out a hand, palm flat and down, and said something to me in his Indian talk and pointed far off to the east and south and back again to me and reached inside the old blanket he had fastened around him with a belt and took out a dirty cloth-wrapped package and laid it at my feet, and went away and faded

42

out of sight around the shack. When I unrolled that package there were those moccasins.

Funny thing. I never wanted to go around telling my story to the other boys again. Didn't need to. Whether they believed or not wasn't important any more. I had those moccasins. In a way they made me one of Jacob's children. Remembering that has helped me sometimes in tough spots.

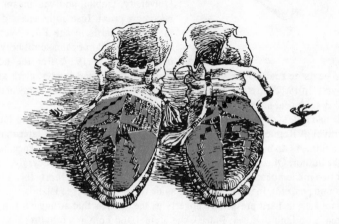

Liam O'Flaherty

Liam O'Flaherty was born in 1897 on Inishmore, one of the Aran Islands off the coast of Galway. He was educated at Catholic schools and the National University, Dublin, and was meant to become a priest. Instead he enlisted in the Irish Guards in the First World War and fought in France until he was invalided out in 1917. For the next three years he roamed the world, working as a deck-hand, porter, clerk and labourer. In 1922 he returned to Dublin to fight for the Republican Army in the Civil War. A year later he went to London to write.

He had little success until the publication of *The Informer* in 1925. This lurid portrayal of Republican terrorism received wide acclaim and was later made into a film. As do his other novels, it reflected the attraction that violence held for the author. Of his first, unpublished, effort, he once commented wryly, "At least two million people were killed in it." By comparison, his short stories are quiet and peaceful. In them, he returns again to the barren Aran Islands, whose peasants are as hard pressed by poverty as the animals that struggle for their existence on land and sea. Indeed, the animal and human worlds seem very close. The wild goat's fearless defence of her offspring in THE WILD GOAT'S KID is comparable to the unthinking recklessness of the bird-catcher risking his life on the cliffs in *Trapped* or the quick-witted instinct for self-preservation and rivalry demonstrated by the old man in *A Shilling*. These and other stories can be found in a number of anthologies.

Since 1935 Liam O'Flaherty has lived mainly in America and has written little.

The Wild Goat's Kid

by Liam O'Flaherty

Her nimble hoofs made music on the crags all winter, as she roamed along the cliff-tops over the sea.

During the previous autumn, when goats were mating, she had wandered away, one of a small herd that trotted gaily after a handsome fellow, with a splendid grey-black hide and winding horns. It was her first mating. Then, with the end of autumn, peasant boys came looking for their goats. The herd was broken up. The gallant buck was captured and slain by two hungry dogs from the village of Drumranny. The white goat alone remained. She had wandered too far away from her master's village. He couldn't find her. She was given up as lost.

So that she became a wild one of the cliffs, where the seagulls and the cormorants were lords, and the great eagle of Mohur soared high over the thundering sea. Her big, soft, yellow eyes became wild from looking down often at the sea, with her long chin whiskers swaying gracefully in the wind. She was a long, slender thing, with short, straight horns and ringlets of matted hair trailing far down on either haunch.

With her tail in the air, snorting, tossing her horns, she fled when anybody approached. Her hoofs would patter over the crags until she was far away. Then she would stand on some eminence and turn about to survey the person who had disturbed her, calmly, confident in the power of her slender legs to carry her beyond pursuit.

She roamed at will. No stone fence however high could resist her long leap, as she sprang on muscular thighs that bent like silk.

45

She was so supple that she could trot on the top of a thin fence, carelessly, without a sound except the gentle tapping of her delicate hoofs. She hardly ever left the cliff-tops. There was plenty of food there, for the winter was mild, and the leaves and grasses that grew between the crevices of the crags were flavoured by the strong, salt taste of the brine carried up on the wind. She grew sleek and comely.

Towards the end of winter a subtle change came over her. Her hearing became more acute. She took fright at the least sound. She began to shun the sea except on very calm days, when it did not roar. She ate less. She grew very particular about what she ate. She hunted around a long time before she chose a morsel. She often went on her knees, reaching down into the bottom of a crevice to nibble at a briar that was inferior to the more accessible ones. She became corpulent. Her udder increased.

Winter passed. Green leaves began to sprout. Larks sang in the morning. There was sweetness in the air and a great urge of life. The white goat, one morning a little after dawn, gave birth to a grey-black kid.

The kid was born in a tiny, green glen under an overhanging ledge of low rock that sheltered it from the wind. It was a male kid, an exquisite, fragile thing, tinted delicately with many colours. His slender belly was milky white. The insides of his thighs were of the same colour. He had deep rings of grey, like bracelets, above his hoofs. He had black kneecaps on his forelegs, like pads, to protect him when he knelt to take his mother's teats into his silky, black mouth. His back and sides were grey-black. His ears were black, long, and drooping with the weakness of infancy.

The white goat bleated over him, with soft eyes and shivering flanks, gloating over the exquisite thing that had been created within her by the miraculous power of life. And she had this delicate creature all to herself, in the wild solitude of the beautiful little glen, within earshot of the murmuring sea, with little birds whistling their spring songs around about her, and the winds coming with their slow murmurs over the crags. The first tender hours of her first motherhood were undisturbed by any restraint, not even by the restraint of a mate's presence. In absolute freedom and quiet, she watched with her young.

How she manoeuvred to make him stand! She breathed on him to warm him. She raised him gently with her forehead, uttering strange, soft sounds to encourage him. Then he stood up, trembling, staggering, swaying on his curiously long legs. She became very excited, rushing around him, bleating nervously, afraid that he should fall again. He fell. She was in agony. Bitter wails came from her distended jaws and she crunched her teeth. But she renewed her efforts, urging the kid to rise, to rise and live . . . to live, live, live.

He rose again. Now he was steadier. He shook his head. He wagged his long ears as his mother breathed into them. He took a few staggering steps, came to his padded knees, and rose again immediately. Slowly, gently, gradually, she pushed him towards her udder with her horns. At last he took the teat within his mouth, he pushed joyously, sank to his knees and began to drink.

She stayed with him all day in the tiny glen, just nibbling a few mouthfuls of the short grass that grew around. Most of the time she spent exercising her kid. With a great show of anxiety and importance, she brought him on little expeditions across the glen

to the opposite rock, three yards away and back again. At first he staggered clumsily against her sides, and his tiny hoofs often lost their balance on tufts of grass, such was his weakness. But he gained strength with amazing speed, and the goat's joy and pride increased. She suckled and caressed him after each tiny journey.

When the sun had set he was able to walk steadily, to take little short runs, to toss his head. They lay all night beneath the shelter of the ledge, with the kid between his mother's legs, against her warm udder.

Next morning she hid him securely in a crevice of the neighbouring crag, in a small groove between two flags that were covered with a withered growth of wild grass and ferns. The kid crawled instinctively into the warm hole without any resistance to the gentle push of his mother's horns. He lay down with his head towards his doubled hind legs, and closed his eyes. Then the goat scraped the grass and fern-stalks over the entrance hole with her fore feet, and she hurried away to graze, as carelessly as if she had no kid hidden.

All the morning, as she grazed hurriedly and fiercely around the crag, she took great pains to pretend that she was not aware of her kid's nearness. Even when she grazed almost beside the hiding-place, she never noticed him, by look or by cry. But still, she pricked her little ears at every distant sound.

At noon she took him out and gave him suck. She played with him on a grassy knoll and watched him prance about. She taught him how to rear on his hind legs and fight the air with his forehead. Then she put him back into his hiding-place and returned to graze. She continued to graze until nightfall.

Just when she was about to fetch him from his hole and take him to the overhanging ledge to rest for the night, a startling sound reached her ears. It came from afar, from the south, from beyond a low fence that ran across the crag on the skyline. It was indistinct, barely audible, a deep, purring sound. But to the ears of the mother-goat, it was loud and ominous as a thunderclap. It was the heavy breathing of a dog sniffing the wind.

She listened stock-still, with her head in the air and her short tail lying stiff along her back, twitching one ear. The sound came again. It was nearer. Then there was a patter of feet. Then a clumsy, black figure hurtled over the fence and dropped on to the crag, with awkward secrecy. The goat saw a black dog, a large, curly fellow, standing by the fence in the dim twilight, with his fore paw raised and his long, red tongue hanging. Then he shut his mouth suddenly, and raising his snout upwards sniffed several times, contracting his nostrils as he did so, as if in pain. Then he whined savagely, and trotted towards the goat sideways.

She snorted. It was a sharp, dull thud, like a blow from a rubber sledge. Then she rapped the crag three times with her left fore foot, loudly and sharply. The dog stood still and raised his fore paw again. He bent down his head and looked at her with narrowed eyes. Then he licked his breast and began to run swiftly to the left. He was running towards the kid's hiding-place, with his tail stretched out straight and his snout to the wind.

49

With another fierce snort the goat charged him at full speed, in order to cut him off from his advance on the kid's hiding-place. He stopped immediately when she charged. The goat halted, too, five yards from the hiding-place, facing the dog.

The dog stood still. His eyes wandered around in all directions, with the bashfulness of a sly brute, caught suddenly in an awkward position. Then slowly he raised his bloodshot eyes to the goat. He bared his fangs. His mane rose like a fan. His tail shot out. Picking his steps like a lazy cat, he approached her without a sound. The goat shivered along her left flank, and she snorted twice in rapid succession.

When he was within six yards of her he uttered a ferocious roar—a deep, rumbling sound in his throat. He raced towards her, and leaped clean into the air, as if she were a fence that he was trying to vault. She parried him subtly with her horns, like a swordthrust, without moving her fore feet. Her sharp horns just grazed his belly as he whizzed past her head. But the slight blow deflected his course. Instead of falling on his feet, as he had intended cunningly to do, between the goat and the kid, he was thrown to the left and fell on his side, with a thud. The goat whirled about and charged him.

But he had risen immediately and jerked himself away, with his haunches low down, making a devilish scraping and yelping and growling noise. He wanted to terrify the kid out of his hiding-place. Then it would be easy to overpower the goat, hampered by the task of hiding the kid between her legs.

The kid uttered a faint, querulous cry, but the goat immediately replied with a sharp, low cry. The kid mumbled something indistinct, and then remained silent. There was a brushing sound among the ferns that covered him. He was settling himself down farther. The goat trotted rigidly to the opposite side of the hiding-place to face the dog again.

The dog had run away some distance, and lay on his belly, licking his paws. Now he meant to settle himself down properly to the prolonged attack, after the failure of his first onslaught. He yawned lazily and made peculiar mournful noises, thrusting his head into the air and twitching his snout. The goat watched every single movement and sound, with her ears thrust forward past her horns. Her great, soft eyes were very wild and timorous in spite of the valiant posture of her body, and the terrific force of the blows she delivered occasionally on the hard crag with her little hoofs.

The dog remained lying for half an hour or so, continuing his weird pantomime. The night fell completely. Everything became unreal and ghostly under the light of the distant myriads of stars. An infant moon had arisen. The sharp rushing wind and the thunder of the sea only made the silent loneliness of the night more menacing to the white goat, as she stood bravely on the limestone crag defending her newborn young. On all sides the horizon was a tumultuous line of barren crag, dented with shallow glens and seamed with low, stone fences that hung like tattered curtains against the rim of the sky.

Then the dog attacked again. Rising suddenly, he set off at a long, swinging gallop, with his head turned sideways towards the goat, whining as he ran. He ran around the goat in a wide circle, gradually increasing his speed. A white spot on his breast flashed and vanished as he rose and fell in the undulating stretches of his flight. The goat watched him, fiercely rigid from tail to snout. She pawed the crag methodically, turning around on her own ground slowly to face him.

When he passed his starting-point, he was flying at full speed, a black ball shooting along the gloomy surface of the crag, with a sharp rattle of claws. The rattle of his claws, his whining and the sharp tapping of the goat's fore feet as she turned about, were the only sounds that rose into the night from this sinister engagement.

He sped round and round the goat, approaching her imperceptibly each round, until he was so close that she could see his glittering eyes and the white lather of rage on his half-open jaws. She became slightly dizzy and confused, turning about so methodically in a confined space, confused and amazed by the subtle strategy of the horrid beast. His whining grew louder and more savage. The rattle of his claws was like the clamour of hailstones driven by a wind. He was upon her.

He came in a whirl on her flank. He came with a savage roar that deafened her. She shivered and then stiffened in rigid silence to receive him. The kid uttered a shrill cry. Then the black bulk hurtled through the air, close up, with hot breathing, snarling, with reddened fangs and . . . smash.

He had dived for her left flank. But as he went past her head she turned like lightning and met him again with her horns. This time she grazed his side, to the rear of the shoulder. He yelped and tumbled sideways, rolling over twice. With a savage snort she was upon him. He was on his haunches, rising, when her horns thudded into his head. He went down again with another yelp. He rolled over and then suddenly, with amazing speed, swept to his feet, whirled about on swinging tail and dived for her flank once more. The goat uttered a shriek of terror. He had passed her horns. His fangs had embedded themselves in the matted ringlet that trailed along her right flank. The dog's flying weight, swinging on to the ringlet as he fell, brought her to her haunches.

But she was ferocious now. As she wriggled to her feet beside the rolling dog that gripped her flank, she wrenched herself around and gored him savagely in the belly. He yelled and loosed his hold. She rose on her hind legs in a flash, and with a snort she gored him again. Her sharp, pointed horns penetrated his side between the ribs. He gasped and shook his four feet in the air. Then she pounded on him with her fore feet, beating his prostrate body furiously. Her little hoofs pattered with tremendous speed for almost a minute. She beat him blindly, without looking at him.

Then she suddenly stopped. She snorted. The dog was still. She shivered and looked down at him curiously. He was dead. Her terror was passed. She lifted her right fore foot and shook it with a curious movement. Then she uttered a wild, joyous cry and ran towards her kid's hiding-place.

Night passed into a glorious dawn that came over a rippling sea from the east. A wild, sweet dawn, scented with dew and the many perfumes of the germinating earth. The sleepy sun rose brooding from the sea, golden and soft, searching far horizons with its concave shafts of light. The dawn was still. Still and soft and pure.

The white goat and her kid were travelling eastwards along the cliff-tops over the sea. They had travelled all night, flying from the horrid carcass of the beast that lay stretched on the crag beside the little glen. Now they were far away, on the summit of the giant white Precipice of Cahir. The white goat rested to give suck to her kid, and to look out over the cliff-top at the rising sun.

Then she continued her flight eastwards, pushing her tired kid gently before her with her horns.

Kurt Vonnegut Jr.

Kurt Vonnegut was born in 1922 in Indianapolis. During the Second World War he was captured by the Germans and spent five months in a prison camp at Dresden. There he witnessed the bombing of Dresden by the Allies, an event he recreates in several of his books. After the war he studied at the University of Chicago, worked as a reporter and public relations writer, and was soon successful in selling his short stories to magazines. His first novel was published in 1960. Since then he has produced six more novels, two collections of short stories and a number of plays.

Although almost all his work can be described as science fiction, it has little to do with adventures in outer space, ray guns or bug-eyed monsters. Instead, he uses the genre to comment on the nature of Man, social problems or philosophical concepts. HARRISON BERGERON, for example, deals with the idea of equality. But, as you will see in this story, he often treats issues, even such serious ones as political tyranny, in a humorous, satirical fashion. His first book, *Player Piano*, is a biting piece of science fiction satire on the subject of automation. One of his best known novels, *Cat's Cradle*, concerns a new chemical that threatens to destroy the world; among other things it satirises what he feels is the irresponsibility of some scientists; it also takes an ironical look at religion. *Slaughterhouse Five*, another widely acclaimed novel, is concerned with Man's addiction to warfare.

Before tackling these full-length novels, you may prefer to sample more of Kurt Vonnegut's short stories. A selection of these can be found in *Welcome to the Monkey House* and *Cathouse Canary*.

Harrison Bergeron

by Kurt Vonnegut Jr.

The year was 2081, and everybody was finally equal. They weren't only equal before God and the law, they were equal every which way. Nobody was smarter than anybody else; nobody was stronger or quicker than anybody else. All this equality was due to the 211th, 212th, and 213th Amendments to the Constitution, and to the unceasing vigilance of agents of the United States Handicapper General.

Some things about living still weren't quite right, though. April, for instance, still drove people crazy by not being spring-time. And it was in that clammy month that the H-G men took George and Hazel Bergeron's fourteen-year-old son, Harrison, away.

It was tragic, all right, but George and Hazel couldn't think about it very hard. Hazel had a perfectly average intelligence, which meant she couldn't think about anything except in short bursts. And George, while his intelligence was way above normal, had a little mental handicap radio in his ear—he was required by law to wear it at all times. It was tuned to a government transmitter, and every twenty seconds or so, the transmitter would send out some sharp noise to keep people like George from taking unfair advantage of their brains.

George and Hazel were watching television. There were tears on Hazel's cheeks, but she'd forgotten for the moment what they were about, as the ballerinas came to the end of a dance.

A buzzer sounded in George's head. His thoughts fled in panic, like bandits from a burglar alarm.

"That was a real pretty dance, that dance they just did," said Hazel.

"Huh?" said George.

"That dance—it was nice," said Hazel.

"Yup," said George. He tried to think a little about the ballerinas. They weren't really very good—no better than anybody else would have been, anyway. They were burdened with sashweights and bags of birdshot, and their faces were masked, so that no one, seeing a free and graceful gesture or a pretty face, would feel like something the cat dragged in. George was toying with the vague notion that maybe dancers shouldn't be handicapped. But he didn't get very far with it before another noise in his ear radio scattered his thoughts.

George winced. So did two out of the eight ballerinas.

Hazel saw him wince. Having no mental handicap herself, she had to ask George what the latest sound had been.

"Sounded like somebody hitting a milk bottle with a ball-peen hammer," said George.

"I'd think it would be real interesting, hearing all the different sounds," said Hazel, a little envious. "The things they think up."

"Um," said George.

"Only, if I was Handicapper General, you know what I would do?" said Hazel. Hazel, as a matter of fact, bore a strong resemblance to the Handicapper General, a woman named Diana Moon Glampers. "If I was Diana Moon Glampers," said Hazel, "I'd have chimes on Sunday—just chimes. Kind of in honour of religion."

"I could think, if it was just chimes," said George.

"Well—maybe make 'em real loud," said Hazel. "I think I'd make a good Handicapper General."

"Good as anybody else," said George.

"Who knows better'n I do what normal is?" said Hazel.

"Right," said George. He began to think glimmeringly about his abnormal son who was now in jail, about Harrison, but a twenty-one gun salute in his head stopped that.

"Boy!" said Hazel, "that was a doozy, wasn't it?"

It was such a doozy that George was white and trembling, and tears stood on the rims of his red eyes. Two of the eight ballerinas

had collapsed on the studio floor, were holding their temples.

"All of a sudden you look so tired," said Hazel. "Why don't you stretch out on the sofa, so's you can rest your handicap bag on the pillows, honeybunch." She was referring to the forty-seven pounds of birdshot in a canvas bag, which was padlocked around George's neck. "Go on and rest the bag for a little while," she said. "I don't care if you're not equal to me for a while."

George weighed the bag with his hands. "I don't mind it," he said. "I don't notice it any more. It's just part of me."

"You been so tired lately—kind of wore out," said Hazel. "If there was just some way we could make a little hole in the bottom of the bag, and just take out a few of them lead balls. Just a few."

"Two years in prison and two thousand dollars fine for every ball I took out," said George. "I don't call that a bargain."

"If you could just take a few out when you came home from work," said Hazel. "I mean—you don't compete with anybody around here. You just sit around."

"If I tried to get away with it," said George, "then other people'd get away with it—and pretty soon we'd be right back to the dark ages again, with everybody competing against everybody else. You wouldn't like that, would you?"

"I'd hate it," said Hazel.

"There you are," said George. "The minute people start cheating on laws, what do you think happens to society?"

If Hazel hadn't been able to come up with an answer to this question, George couldn't have supplied one. A siren was going off in his head.

"Reckon it'd fall all apart," said Hazel.

"What would?" said George blankly.

"Society," said Hazel uncertainly. "Wasn't that what you just said?"

"Who knows?" said George.

The television programme was suddenly interrupted for a news bulletin. It wasn't clear at first as to what the bulletin was about, since the announcer, like all announcers, had a serious speech impediment. For about half a minute, and in a state of high excitement, the announcer tried to say, "Ladies and gentlemen—"

He finally gave up, handed the bulletin to a ballerina to read.

"That's all right," Hazel said of the announcer, "he tried. That's the big thing. He tried to do the best he could with what God gave him. He should get a nice raise for trying so hard."

"Ladies and gentlemen—" said the ballerina, reading the bulletin. She must have been extraordinarily beautiful, because the mask she wore was hideous. And it was easy to see that she was the strongest and most graceful of all the dancers, for her handicap bags were as big as those worn by two-hundred-pound men.

And she had to apologise at once for her voice, which was a very unfair voice for a woman to use. Her voice was a warm, luminous, timeless melody. "Excuse me—" she said, and she began again, making her voice absolutely uncompetitive.

"Harrison Bergeron, age fourteen," she said in a grackle squawk, "has just escaped from jail, where he was held on suspicion of plotting to overthrow the government. He is a genius

58

and an athlete, is under-handicapped, and is extremely dangerous."

A police photograph of Harrison Bergeron was flashed on the screen—upside down, then sideways, upside down again, then right-side up. The picture showed the full length of Harrison against a background calibrated in feet and inches. He was exactly seven feet tall.

The rest of Harrison's appearance was Halloween and hardware. Nobody had ever borne heavier handicaps. He had outgrown hindrances faster than the H-G men could think them up. Instead of a little ear radio for a mental handicap, he wore a tremendous pair of earphones, and spectacles with thick, wavy lenses besides. The spectacles were intended not only to make him half blind, but to give him whanging headaches besides.

Scrap metal was hung all over him. Ordinarily, there was a certain symmetry, a military neatness to the handicaps issued to strong people, but Harrison looked like a walking junkyard. In the race of life, Harrison carried three hundred pounds.

And to offset his good looks, the H-G men required that he wear at all times a red rubber ball for a nose, keep his eyebrows shaved off, and cover his even white teeth with black caps at snaggle-tooth random.

"If you see this boy," said the ballerina, "do not—I repeat, do not—try to reason with him."

There was the shriek of a door being torn from its hinges.

Screams and barking cries of consternation came from the television set. The photograph of Harrison Bergeron on the screen jumped again and again, as though dancing to the tune of an earthquake.

George Bergeron correctly identified the earthquake, and well he might have—for many was the time his own home had danced to the same crushing tune. "My God!" said George. "That must be Harrison!"

The realisation was blasted from his mind instantly by the sound of an automobile collision in his head.

When George could open his eyes again, the photograph of Harrison was gone. A living, breathing Harrison filled the screen.

Clanking, clownish, and huge, Harrison stood in the centre of the studio. The knob of the uprooted studio door was still in his hand. Ballerinas, technicians, musicians and announcers cowered on their knees before him, expecting to die.

"I am the Emperor!" cried Harrison. "Do you hear? I am the Emperor! Everybody must do what I say at once!" He stamped his foot and the studio shook.

"Even as I stand here," he bellowed, "crippled, hobbled, sickened—I am a greater ruler than any man who ever lived! Now watch me become what I *can* become!"

Harrison tore the straps of his handicap harness like wet tissue paper, tore straps guaranteed to support five thousand pounds.

Harrison's scrap-iron handicaps crashed to the floor.

Harrison thrust his thumbs under the bar of the padlock that secured his head harness. The bar snapped like celery. Harrison smashed his headphones and spectacles against the wall.

He flung away his rubber-ball nose, revealed a man that would have awed Thor, the god of thunder.

"I shall now select my Empress!" he said, looking down on the cowering people. "Let the first woman who dares rise to her feet claim her mate and her throne!"

A moment passed, and then a ballerina arose, swaying like a willow.

Harrison plucked the mental handicap from her ear, snapped off her physical handicaps with marvellous delicacy. Last of all, he removed her mask.

She was blindingly beautiful.

"Now—" said Harrison, taking her hand. "Shall we show the people the meaning of the word dance? Music!" he commanded.

The musicians scrambled back into their chairs, and Harrison stripped them of their handicaps, too. "Play your best," he told them, "and I'll make you barons and dukes and earls."

The music began. It was normal at first—cheap, silly, false. But Harrison snatched two musicians from their chairs, waved them like batons as he sang the music as he wanted it played. He slammed them back into their chairs.

The music began again, and was much improved.

Harrison and his Empress merely listened to the music for a while—listened gravely, as though synchronising their heartbeats

with it.

They shifted their weight to their toes.

Harrison placed his big hands on the girl's tiny waist, letting her sense the weightlessness that would soon be hers.

And then, in an explosion of joy and grace, into the air they sprang!

Not only were the laws of the land abandoned, but the law of gravity and the laws of motion as well.

They reeled, whirled, swivelled, flounced, capered, gambolled and spun.

They leaped like deer on the moon.

The studio ceiling was thirty feet high, but each leap brought the dancers nearer to it.

It became their obvious intention to kiss the ceiling.

They kissed it.

And then, neutralising gravity with love and pure will, they remained suspended in air inches below the ceiling, and they kissed each other for a long, long time.

It was then that Diana Moon Glampers, the Handicapper General, came into the studio with a double-barrelled ten-gauge shotgun. She fired twice, and the Emperor and the Empress were dead before they hit the floor.

Diana Moon Glampers loaded the gun again. She aimed it at the musicians and told them they had ten seconds to get their handicaps back on.

It was then that the Bergerons' television tube burned out.

Hazel turned to comment about the blackout to George. But George had gone out into the kitchen for a can of beer.

George came back in with the beer, paused while a handicap signal shook him up. And then he sat down again. "You been crying?" he said to Hazel, watching her wipe her tears.

"Yup," she said.

"What about?" he said.

"I forget," she said. "Something real sad on television."

"What was it?" he said.

"It's all kind of mixed up in my mind," said Hazel.

"Forget sad things," said George.

"I always do," said Hazel.

"That's my girl," said George. He winced. There was the sound of a riveting gun in his head.

"Gee—I could tell that one was a doozy," said Hazel.

"You can say that again," said George.

"Gee—" said Hazel—"I could tell that one was a doozy."

Colin Thiele

Colin Thiele was born in 1920 at Eudunda in South Australia. He was educated at various country schools, went to Adelaide University and during the Second World War served in the Royal Australian Air Force. After the war he became a teacher and has remained in education ever since.

He has scripted material for radio and television, written fact and fiction for adults, lectured on Australian literature, edited anthologies of verse, drama and prose and produced several volumes of poetry. It is for his children's stories, however, that he is best known. These provide not only humour, as in THE FISH SCALES, but evocative description and a strong sense of drama, of which THE SHELL is a good example. Both these stories are taken from *The Rim of The Morning*, which also contains *Storm Boy*. This moving tale of a young boy who befriends a pelican has recently been made into a film.

Sun on the Stubble—a comedy of Australian farm life—tells of a boy's last year in the country before going to secondary school in the city. *February Dragon* deals with the ever-present danger of bush fires in Australia. *Blue Fin* is about tuna fishing (Colin Thiele has sailed with the tuna fleets in South Australia) and the adventures of an unfortunate ugly duckling of a boy called Snook. Tall, clumsy, ungainly, it is only as a last resort that he is taken along as a crew member on his father's tuna clipper. When disaster strikes, Snook and his badly injured father are left alone on the battered vessel and it is up to Snook to save their lives, their boat and their cargo.

The Shell

by Colin Thiele

The green sea swept into the shallows and seethed there like slaking quicklime. It surged over the rocks, tossing up spangles of water like a juggler and catching them deftly again behind. It raced knee-deep through the clefts and crevices, twisted and tortured in a thousand ways, till it swept nuzzling and sucking into the holes at the base of the cliff. The whole reef was a shambles of foam, but it was bright in the sun, bright as a shattered mirror, exuberant and leaping with light.

No wonder the woman on the tiny white beach in the tuck of the cliffs pressed her sun-glasses close and puckered the corners of her eyes into creases. Before her, the last wave flung itself forward up the slope of the beach, straining and stretched to the utmost, and then, just failing, slid back slowly like a boy on his stomach slipping backwards down the steep face of a gable roof.

The shell lay in a saucer of rock. It was a green cowrie, clean and new, its pink undersides as delicate as human flesh. All round it the rock dropped away sheer or leaned out in an overhang streaked with dripping strands of slime like wet hair. The waves spumed over it, hissing and curling, but the shell tumbled the water off its back or just rocked gently like a bead in the palm of the hand. Its clean gleam caught the woman's eye as she squinted seawards, and her heart stirred acquisitively. It was something she could wade out for when the tide went back; a way of bringing the sea right into the living-room. Just one shell to give artistic balance to her specimen shelf for parties or bridge afternoons with her friends.

Another sea stood up, way out, green and sloping like a railway embankment. It moved forward silently—an immense, mile-long glissade of water coming on inexorably like a sentient thing. The slope steepened, straightened, rose up sheer. And then, almost without warning, it suddenly arched, curled over, and pitched down with a thunder that shook the cliffs and set the shallows leaping and seething again. The rocks seemed to shrug and rise, smothered and streaming; and again the outstretched hurl of the last ripples mouthed the sand at her feet.

She drew back the edges of the rug and straightened the gay canvas umbrella. The hamper-case was folded cleverly into a low table, and for the things inside there was shade enough on the rug: thermos and plastic cups, cold meat, and the green and red of lettuce-wrapped tomatoes. Good food and drink, a hot day, and the elemental companionship of the sea. She stood up and waved: "Oohoo! Harold! David!"

The sounds were gripped, bruised, swept away by the sea-tumult, but the two figures high on the cliff caught her movement and waved back. They pulled in their fishing lines and came slowly down the steep path, wicker-baskets dangling and bumping from their shoulders as they walked. Nearer, round the cliff buttress, they emerged more clearly. The man was tall and thin, with a moustache and skin too white for a place like this. But the fish scales on his coat shone like sequins, and he walked proudly. The boy was the son of his father—twelve or thirteen years old and as thin as a stick. But he swaggered with his basket, trying to look like a veteran.

"Any luck?" The woman held up her hand and crooked its fingertips in the man's as he sat down.

"Two nice sweep. Five-pounders, I'd say. And David nearly got a beauty; had him half-way up, but he dropped off."

The boy made excuses. "It's these hooks! They wouldn't hold an earthworm if it kicked!"

His father flung back the wicker lid and the blue gleam of the fish suddenly caught the sun. "Look!"

"Oh, lovely, dear! We'll have one for tea."

"Wait and see what we get this afternoon. They'll be fresher; I'm going down on to the bottom ledge."

"Do be careful, darling."

"I've watched it all the morning. Not a wave within six feet of it. And it's better fishing—you don't lose so many."

He sprawled out lazily and took the cup from her hand. "Lovely spot! I used to come here when I was a lad."

The boy chortled. "However did you get here *then*?" He laughed. A thin, reedy laugh, pale and watery like his eyes.

"The roads haven't changed much. But we walked or rode horses down here in those days, instead of trying to use cars." He smiled at the memory, even while he kept on munching his lunch.

Two gulls launched themselves from the cliffs and swung above them idly, legs thrust back and wings motionless, cupped and cushioned on air. Then they came in to land, running, and stopped two yards short of them, with a benign expression of unconcern. The boy threw a crust. It fell short, but the gull shuffled in towards him sideways, whipped it up at a thrust, and walked back sedately to safety.

The boy scuffed the sand impatiently with his feet, but his mother sighed and leaned back on her arms. "Even the gulls are dignified."

"I can't understand why more people don't come here," the boy said.

"I'm glad they don't."

The man laughed mirthlessly. "They will! Port Lincoln's only twenty miles away."

"Painters and poets should come first," his wife said with sudden feeling; "to see all this before the vandals come, with rifles and bottles."

The man looked out across the leaping foam, puckering his eyes. "There are no seascapes like this east of the Bight. Cape Carnot, Redbanks, Wanna. Giddying cliffs for the climber, and big fish for the liar."

But the boy was kicking moodily at the sand. "I've finished, Mum. Can I go for a walk on the headland?"

"David, dear, can't you sit still for a second while we finish our lunch?"

"Can I?"

67

"There are some very high cliffs along there. They drop sheer into the sea."

"Can I? Please?"

"No, it's too dangerous."

"Arh-h, gosh! Look where we've been fishing all the morning . . . on a little ledge."

"But your father was with you then."

The boy turned to the man, wheedling. "Ah-h, can't I, Dad?"

The man pushed uncomfortably at the sand with the sole of his sandal. "Well . . . just to the top of the headland."

She felt she'd been let down. "Harold!"

"Let him go, Ethel, if it makes him happy. It'll only take five minutes, and we'll be able to watch him all the way."

The boy dashed off around the curve of the beach, his hair brushed up by the wind. The man and the woman lay idle and silent, looking across the bay to the line of cliffs beyond, where the coast curved round from cape to cape, southwards towards Sleaford and Thistle Island and Cape Catastrophe. Everywhere great columns of white spray rose as if in slow motion, like bunches of lace thrust up in fistfuls from below.

"It's never still," she said slowly.

"Looks for all the world like exploding depth-charges. Like some coot rolling them off the cliffs for fun."

She sniffed. "What a comparison! You men!"

"They make nearly as much noise, too. Shake the cliffs. Up on the ledge you can feel them vibrating."

"They must bring in some beautiful shells. There's one in that rock just there, see. I'm going to get it later."

"Vanity! Native races use them for money."

"What if they do. This is a gift to me from the sea."

He smiled weakly. "I read somewhere that we take too much from the sea and give nothing back."

"It always seems to have plenty to spare."

He laughed. "Yes, it can take as well as give. It's old enough to look after itself."

She gazed at the great line of breakers, unsmiling. "One shipwreck would be worth a million shells."

"Perhaps when it feels that the ledger is getting out of balance it just helps itself again."

She folded the cloth, flicking off the crumbs. He brushed the sand from his arms and stood up. "Well, back to the fish!"

"Don't be too long, dear," she said. "We have to leave by four."

"Whatever for?"

"Mrs. Harvery's asked us out to bridge tonight. Remember?"

"What, again?" His voice carried his irritation. "Fancy having to play bridge in a room with walls . . . after *this*." He strode off up the path. The boy, who was on his way back from the headland, ran to catch him up.

Back on the cliff-tops again, he took up his bait box and lines. Then, guiding the boy, he climbed down very carefully to the lowest shelf. "Easy now, son! Watch your step here." The boy was afraid, but he would never have admitted it to his father. "Gosh, it's steep. You feel as if you're hanging out over the water."

"You are in some places. Don't look down until we reach the ledge."

When they got there the boy was surprised to see how big it was—a wide, flat slab of rock jutting out like a balcony, warm as an ovenplate in the afternoon sun. "It's beaut, Dad!"

"Good spot! I've often fished here."

"Catch much?"

"Lovely sweep. Rock cod, of course. Even snapper sometimes." They sat down with their backs to the cliff and took out their lines. The boy felt as if he was suspended on a platform over a maelstrom, but his father was an old hand at rock fishing and scarcely raised his head. They baited and threw out, far out. The seething foam hissed round their lines with the speed of a shark's rush, and they felt the churn and thud of the water in their hands. They were in touch with turmoil, the shock and fear of it surging up to the boy. But for all that, the tug of a big fish was a stronger pull, firm and evenly sustained. It was on the man's line. He brought it clear of the water, a dark blue sweep dangling perilously above the abyss with the line going straight down into its mouth.

From the beach the woman saw it going up, like a spider

devouring its own thread. She waved and shouted, but their senses were numbed by the crash of the surf. The man hauled the fish on to the ledge, twisted it free, and dropped it into the basket. There it flapped for a while under the lid like a spatter of rain on a roof, until it faltered and weakened and slowly died.

He flung his line back into the water in a wide downward arc where a wave caught it and gulped it under again. This time there were no bites. He leaned back against the cliff behind him, loose but quaintly unbending—a young man not yet stiffly old, an old man still vaguely and youthfully supple. The boy fidgeted with his line for a long time, but at last he leaned back, too. The shock and thud of the water against the cliff was almost peaceful—a sort of incessant clubbing that numbed and drowsed him by its sheer weight and ceaselessness. He looked up at the cliff edge above him where the tussocky clumps hissed and flickered in the sea-wind, and swivelled his head upwards and around at the noiseless sweep of a kestrel passing over. The man looked up, too, gazing beyond the bird into the blue dome of distance beyond. The two of them, man and boy, were peering skywards.

And then, quite suddenly, the sea came and took them. It stood up and plucked them off the ledge swiftly and decisively, like a hand coming up over a shelf for a rag doll. They barely had time to bring their eyes down to it before it stood six feet high on the ledge, clasped them both, and then fell away, sucking and sobbing as it plunged backwards the way it had come.

Some strange and elemental cohesion, a momentary coalescing of mighty forces, suddenly pitched that great wave up beyond its fellows—twenty, thirty feet up out of a regular sea. A few moments later another, and then a third, towered up and roared high against the rock wall, shooting flares of spray over the topmost edge and drenching the bitter salt-white herbage of the cliff-top. Then, as if satisfied with its random muscle-flexing, the sea sank back into its rhythms again like a tigress dozing in the sunshine.

Down in the bay the woman sprang back with a vexed cry as the first big wave seethed in low about her, nosing the sand as if sensing prey. It pummelled her feet, tumbled the gay umbrella on its side, and floated her rug back down the slope of the beach like

loot. She ran forward quickly, checked it with her foot, and dragged it to safety, sodden and sand-streaked. Then, on an impulse, she turned and looked up at the ledge on the cliff. It was bare. Water was streaming from it in rivulets, in thick sinewy ropes, in feathery wisps—all falling downwards, downwards, and slowly dying away.

"Harold! David!"

Her scream caught a momentary lull between waves and shrilled out over the little bay. She ran up the steep path in a frenzy, stumbling over rocks and hollows.

"Harold! Harold! David.... Oh, David-d-d!"

She reached the cliff-top, sobbing and gulping for breath, and rushed forward to stare down on to the ledge. But the last of the huge waves had just come and receded, and the ledge was a slab of clean, dark rock, gleaming like a new tombstone of black marble. It was empty. Only over one corner a single fishing-line still ran, bellying out a little and thrumming intermittently in the wind. Two or three glistening drops, shaken clear of it, fell back into the sea like beads.

"Harold! David-d-d! Oh, my God!"

Two gulls, alarmed by her cries, rose effortlessly and hung above her, above the ledge, above the abyss in ironic dumb-show, their legs thrust back and their pink eyes looking down at her, coldly disinterested. Yet perhaps, in their relentless way, they saw more than she.

"They always come in threes, them big fellows," said the old fisherman from Port Lincoln. "And clean out of the blue. You'd have thought Harold would have known that, bein' born here and all."

The police sergeant walked briskly along the cliffs, saying nothing. It was three hours since a woman, hysterical and incoherent, had collapsed on his doorstep with her story.

"Here it is," said the old man. "This'll be the ledge all right." The sergeant looked over cautiously. "No hope of recovering the bodies down there."

"Not a hope in the world. Not even if we knew where they were. Poor devils."

"Horrible way to die."

The sergeant turned to the two uniformed men with him. "Better search along the little beach—just in case." The constables turned and walked off down the slope, but the old man spat expressively. "Nuh, never find 'em there, Serg. They're down below here—if the sharks haven't got 'em."

Down on the beach the two men searched carefully and fruitlessly. Suddenly one of them stopped and pointed. "Better gather up that picnic gear, Geoff . . . umbrella, rug, hamper, books. . . ."

"Better scout around a bit; it's probably scattered all over the place."

The first man searched down along the shore and stopped near a rock exposed by the ebb. "Look at this shell," he called. "It's a beauty. A green cowrie."

"Never mind about shells. Get the rug."

"I'm taking it home to my wife. These shells are currency in some countries, you know."

"Blood-money! The sea's buying you off!" He watched distastefully as the first man reached down and closed his fingers beneath the smooth pink underside of the shell, as delicate as human flesh. And the sea came gurgling gently round his shoes, like a cat rubbing its back against his legs.

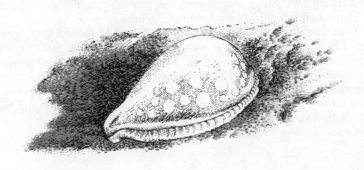

Charles Dickens

Charles Dickens was born in 1812 and grew up in London. His family was always in financial difficulties: his father, a poor and easy-going clerk, was imprisoned as a debtor; his mother's attempts to start a school were unsuccessful; the family furniture was pawned; and at the age of twelve, Dickens himself was sent to work in a factory, pasting labels on bottles of shoe polish. He attended school intermittently until he was fourteen. Shortly afterwards he became a newspaper reporter.

The misery and humiliation he experienced during his childhood left a lasting impression. His early experiences not only provided the basis for many of the characters and events in his books, they also gave him great sympathy for the poor and helpless. In many of his novels, he was concerned with social problems and attacked cruel and unjust laws. But he also had a great gift for comic writing, which he used to good effect in his second book, *The Posthumous Papers of the Pickwick Club*. Published when he was twenty-four, this collection of stories describing the adventures of the Pickwick Club's slightly eccentric members brought him literary fame.

Other books include *Oliver Twist*, *David Copperfield*, *Great Expectations* and *The Old Curiosity Shop*. In them he created some of the most famous characters in English literature—Fagin, Uriah Heep, Mr. Micawber (who was modelled closely on his own father), Miss Haversham and Little Nell. But perhaps his best-known character is Scrooge of *A Christmas Carol*, the miser who is reformed by ghostly visitations. The supernatural also features in THE SIGNALMAN.

Charles Dickens died in 1870.

The Signalman

by Charles Dickens

"Halloa! Below there!"

When he heard a voice thus calling to him, he was standing at the door of his box, with a flag in his hand, furled round its short pole. One would have thought, considering the nature of the ground, that he could not have doubted from what quarter the voice came; but, instead of looking up to where I stood on the top of the steep cutting nearly over his head, he turned himself about and looked down the Line. There was something remarkable in his manner of doing so, though I could not have said, for my life, what. But I know it was remarkable enough to attract my notice, even though his figure was foreshortened and shadowed, down in the deep trench, and mine was high above him, so steeped in the glow of an angry sunset that I had shaded my eyes with my hand before I saw him at all.

"Halloa! Below!"

From looking down the Line, he turned himself about again, and, raising his eyes, saw my figure high above him.

"Is there any path by which I can come down and speak to you?"

He looked up at me without replying, and I looked down at him without pressing him too soon with a repetition of my idle question. Just then there came a vague vibration in the earth and air, quickly changing into a violent pulsation, and an oncoming rush that caused me to start back as though it had force to draw me down. When such vapour as rose to my height from this rapid train, had passed me and was skimming away over the landscape,

I looked down again and saw him refurling the flag he had shown while the train went by.

I repeated my inquiry. After a pause, during which he seemed to regard me with fixed attention, he motioned with his rolled-up flag towards a point on my level, some two or three hundred yards distant. I called down to him, "All right!" and made for that point. There, by dint of looking closely about me, I found a rough zigzag descending path notched out, which I followed.

The cutting was extremely deep and unusually precipitate. It was made through a clammy stone that became oozier and wetter as I went down. For these reasons, I found the way long enough to give me time to recall a singular air of reluctance or compulsion with which he had pointed out the path.

When I came down low enough upon the zigzag descent, to see him again, I saw that he was standing between the rails on the way by which the train had lately passed, in an attitude as if he were waiting for me to appear. He had his left hand at his chin, and that left elbow rested on his right hand crossed over his breast. His attitude was one of such expectation and watchfulness, that I stopped a moment, wondering at it.

I resumed my downward way, and, stepping out upon the level of the railroad and drawing nearer to him, saw that he was a dark, sallow man, with a dark beard and rather heavy eyebrows. His post was in as solitary and dismal a place as ever I saw. On either side, a dripping-wet wall of jagged stone, excluding all view but a strip of sky; the perspective one way, only a crooked prolongation of this great dungeon; the shorter perspective in the other direction terminating in a gloomy red light and the gloomier entrance to a black tunnel, in whose massive architecture there was a barbarous, depressing, and forbidding air. So little sunlight ever found its way to this spot, that it had an earthy, deadly smell; and so much cold wind rushed through it, that it struck chill to me, as if I had left the natural world.

Before he stirred, I was near enough to him to have touched him. Not even then removing his eyes from mine, he stepped back one step and lifted his hand.

This was a lonesome post to occupy (I said), and it had riveted my attention when I looked down from up yonder. A visitor was a rarity, I should suppose; not an unwelcome rarity, I hoped? In me he merely saw a man who had been shut up within narrow limits all his life, and who, being at last set free, had a newly awakened interest in these great works. To such purpose I spoke to him; but I am far from sure of the terms I used, for, besides that I am not happy in opening any conversation, there was something in the man that daunted me.

He directed a most curious look towards the red light near the tunnel's mouth, and looked all about it as if something were missing from it, and then looked at me.

That light was part of his charge? Was it not?

He answered in a low voice: "Don't you know it is?"

The monstrous thought came into my mind as I perused the fixed eyes and the saturnine face, that this was a spirit, not a man. I have speculated since, whether there may have been infection in his mind.

In my turn, I stepped back. But in making the action, I detected in his eyes some latent fear of me. This put the monstrous thought to flight.

"You look at me," I said, forcing a smile, "as if you had a dread of me."

"I was doubtful," he returned, "whether I had seen you before."

"Where?"

He pointed to the red light he had looked at.

"There?" I said.

Intently watchful of me, he replied (but without sound), Yes.

"My good fellow, what should I do there? However, be that as it may, I never was there, you may swear."

"I think I may," he rejoined. "Yes. I am sure I may."

His manner cleared, like my own. He replied to my remarks with readiness and in well-chosen words. Had he much to do there? Yes; that was to say, he had enough responsibility to bear; but exactness and watchfulness were what was required of him, and of actual work—manual labour he had next to none. To change that signal, to trim those lights, and to turn this iron handle now and then, was all he had to do under that head. Regarding those many long and lonely hours of which I seemed to make so much, he could only say that the routine of his life had shaped itself into that form and he had grown used to it. He had taught himself a language down here—if only to know it by sight, and to have formed his own crude ideas of its pronunciation, could be called learning it. He had also worked at fractions and decimals, and tried a little algebra; but he was, and had been as a boy, a poor hand at figures. Was it necessary for him, when on duty, always to remain in that channel of damp air, and could he never rise into the sunshine from between those high stone walls? Why, that

78

depended upon times and circumstances. Under some conditions there would be less upon the Line than under others, and the same held good as to certain hours of the day and night. In bright weather, he did choose occasions for getting a little above these lower shadows; but being at all times liable to be called by his electric bell, and at such times listening for it with redoubled anxiety, the relief was less than I would suppose.

He took me into his box, where there was a fire, a desk for an official book in which he had to make certain entries, a telegraphic instrument with its dial face and needles, and the little bell of which he had spoken. On my trusting that he would excuse the remark that he had been well educated and (I hoped I might say without offence) perhaps educated above that station, he observed that instances of slight incongruity in such-wise would rarely be found wanting among large bodies of men; that he had heard it was so in workhouses, in the police force, even in that last desperate resource, the army; and that he knew it was so, more or less, in any great railway staff. He had been, when young (if I could believe it, sitting in that hut; he scarcely could), a student of natural philosophy and had attended lectures; but he had run wild, misused his opportunities, gone down, and never risen again. He had no complaint to offer about that. He had made his bed, and he lay upon it. It was far too late to make another.

All that I have here condensed, he said in a quiet manner, with his grave dark regards divided between me and the fire. He threw in the word 'Sir' from time to time, and especially when he referred to his youth, as though to request me to understand that he claimed to be nothing but what I found him. He was several times interrupted by the little bell, and had to read off messages and send replies. Once, he had to stand without the door, and display a flag as a train passed, and make some verbal communication to the driver. In the discharge of his duties I observed him to be remarkably exact and vigilant, breaking off his discourse at a syllable and remaining silent until what he had to do was done.

In a word, I should have set this man down as one of the safest of men to be employed in that capacity, but for the circumstance that while he was speaking to me he twice broke off with a fallen colour, turned his face towards the little bell when it did *not* ring,

opened the door of the hut (which was kept shut to exclude the unhealthy damp), and looked out towards the red light near the mouth of the tunnel. On both of those occasions he came back to the fire with the inexplicable air upon him which I had remarked, without being able to define, when we were so far asunder.

Said I when I rose to leave him: "You almost make me think that I have met with a contented man."

(I am afraid I must acknowledge that I said it to lead him on.)

"I believe I used to be so," he rejoined, in the low voice in which he had first spoken; "but I am troubled, sir, I am troubled."

He would have recalled the words if he could. He had said them, however, and I took them up quickly.

"With what? What is your trouble?"

"It is very difficult to impart, sir. It is very, very difficult to speak of. If ever you make me another visit, I will try to tell you."

"But I expressly intend to make you another visit. Say, when shall it be?"

"I go off early in the morning, and I shall be on again at ten tomorrow night, sir."

"I will come at eleven."

He thanked me, and went out at the door with me. "I'll show my white light, sir," he said, in his peculiar low voice, "till you have found the way up. When you have found it, don't call out! And when you are at the top, don't call out!"

His manner seemed to make the place strike colder to me, but I said no more than "Very well".

"And when you come down tomorrow night, don't call out! Let me ask you a parting question. What made you cry 'Halloa! Below there!' tonight?"

"Heaven knows," said I. "I cried something to that effect——"

"Not to that effect, sir. Those were the very words. I know them well."

"Admit those were the very words. I said them, no doubt, because I saw you below."

"For no other reason?"

"What other reason could I possibly have!"

"You had no feeling that they were conveyed to you in any supernatural way?"

"No."

He wished me good night, and held up his light. I walked by the side of the down Line of rails (with a very disagreeable sensation of a train coming behind me), until I found the path. It was easier to mount than to descend, and I got back to my inn without any adventure.

Punctual to my appointment, I placed my foot on the first notch of the zigzag next night, as the distant clocks were striking eleven. He was waiting for me at the bottom, with his white light on. "I have not called out," I said, when we came close together; "may I speak now?" "By all means, sir." "Good night then, and here's my hand." "Good night, sir, and here's mine." With that we walked side by side to his box, entered it, closed the door, and sat down by the fire.

"I have made up my mind, sir," he began, bending forward as soon as we were seated, and speaking in a tone but a little above a whisper, "that you shall not have to ask me twice what troubles me. I took you for someone else yesterday evening. That troubles me."

"That mistake?"

"No. That someone else."

"Who is it?"

"I don't know."

"Like me?"

"I don't know. I never saw the face. The left arm is across the face, and the right arm is waved. Violently waved. This way."

I followed his action with my eyes, and it was the action of an arm gesticulating with the utmost passion and vehemence: "For God's sake clear the way!"

"One moonlight night," said the man, "I was sitting here, when I heard a voice cry 'Halloa! Below there!' I started up, looked from that door, and saw this someone else standing by the red light near the tunnel, waving as I just now showed you. The voice seemed hoarse with shouting, and it cried, 'Look out! Look out!' And then again 'Halloa! Below there! Look out!' I caught up my lamp, turned it on red, and ran towards the figure, calling, 'What's wrong? What has happened? Where?' It stood just outside the blackness of the tunnel. I advanced so close upon it that I wondered at its keeping the sleeve across its eyes. I ran right up at it, and had my hand stretched out to pull the sleeve away, when it was gone."

"Into the tunnel," said I.

"No. I ran on into the tunnel, five hundred yards. I stopped and held my lamp above my head, and saw the figures of the measured distance, and saw the wet stains stealing down the walls and trickling through the arch. I ran out again, faster than I had run in (for I had a mortal abhorrence of the place upon me), and I looked all round the red light with my own red light, and I went up the iron ladder to the gallery atop of it, and I came down again, and ran back here. I telegraphed both ways, 'An alarm has been given. Is anything wrong?' The answer came back, both ways: 'All well'. "

Resisting the slow touch of a frozen finger tracing out my spine, I showed him how that this figure must be a deception of his sense of sight, and how that figures, originating in disease of the delicate nerves that minister to the functions of the eye, were known to have often troubled patients, some of whom had become conscious of the nature of their affliction, and had even proved it by experiments upon themselves. "As to an imaginary cry," said I, "do but listen for a moment to the wind in this unnatural valley while we spoke so low, and to the wild harp it makes of the telegraph wires!"

That was all very well, he returned, after we had sat listening for a while, and he ought to know something of the wind and the wires, he who so often passed long winter nights there, alone and watching. But he would beg to remark that he had not finished.

I asked his pardon, and he slowly added these words, touching my arm:

"Within six hours after the Appearance, the memorable accident on this Line happened, and within ten hours the dead and wounded were brought along through the tunnel over the spot where the figure had stood."

A disagreeable shudder crept over me, but I did my best against it. It was not to be denied, I rejoined, that this was a remarkable coincidence, calculated deeply to impress his mind. But it was unquestionable that remarkable coincidences did continually occur, and they must be taken into account in dealing with such a subject. Though to be sure I must admit, I added (for I thought I saw that he was going to bring the objection to bear upon me), men of common sense did not allow much for coincidences in making the ordinary calculations of life.

He again begged to remark that he had not finished.

I again begged his pardon for being betrayed into interruptions.

"This," he said, again laying his hand upon my arm, and glancing over his shoulder with hollow eyes, "was just a year ago. Six or seven months passed, and I had recovered from the surprise and shock, when one morning, as the day was breaking, I, standing at that door, looked towards the red light and saw the spectre again." He stopped, with a fixed look at me.

"Did it cry out?"

"No. It was silent."

"Did it wave its arm?"

"No. It leaned against the shaft of the light, with both hands before the face. Like this."

Once more I followed his action with my eyes. It was an action of mourning. I have seen such an attitude in stone figures on tombs.

"Did you go up to it?"

"I came in and sat down, partly to collect my thoughts, partly because it had turned me faint. When I went to the door again, daylight was above me, and the ghost was gone."

"But nothing followed? Nothing came of this?"

He touched me on the arm with his forefinger twice or thrice, giving a ghastly nod each time:

"That very day, as a train came out of the tunnel, I noticed, at a carriage window on my side, what looked like a confusion of hands and heads, and something waved. I saw it, just in time to signal the driver, Stop! He shut off, and put his brake on, but the train drifted past here a hundred and fifty yards or more. I ran after it, and, as I went along, heard terrible screams and cries. A beautiful young lady had died instantaneously in one of the compartments, and was brought in here and laid down on this floor between us."

Involuntarily, I pushed my chair back, as I looked from the boards at which he pointed, to himself.

"True, sir. True. Precisely as it happened, so I tell it you."

I could think of nothing to say, to any purpose, and my mouth was very dry. The wind and the wires took up the story with a long lamenting wail.

He resumed. "Now, sir, mark this, and judge how my mind is troubled. The spectre came back, a week ago. Ever since, it has been there, now and again, by fits and starts."

"At the light?"

"At the Danger-light."

"What does it seem to do?"

He repeated, if possible with increased passion and vehemence, that former gesticulation of "For God's sake clear the way!"

Then he went on. "I have no peace or rest for it. It calls to me, for many minutes together, in an agonised manner, 'Below there! Look out! Look out!' It stands waving to me. It rings my little bell——"

I caught at that. "Did it ring your bell yesterday evening when I was here, and you went to the door?"

"Twice."

"Why, see," said I, "how your imagination misleads you. My

eyes were on the bell, my ears were open to the bell, and if I am a living man, it did *not* ring at those times. No, nor at any other time, except when it was rung in the natural course of physical things by the station communicating with you."

He shook his head. "I have never made a mistake as to that, yet, sir. I have never confused the spectre's ring with the man's. The ghost's ring is a strange vibration in the bell that it derives from nothing else, and I have not asserted that the bell stirs to the eye. I don't wonder that you failed to hear it. But *I* heard it."

"And did the spectre seem to be there, when you looked out?"

"It *was* there."

"Both times?"

He repeated firmly: "Both times."

"Will you come to the door with me and look for it now?"

He bit his under-lip as though he were somewhat unwilling, but arose. I opened the door, and stood on the step while he stood in the doorway. There, was the Danger-light. There, was the dismal mouth of the tunnel. There, were the high, wet, stone walls of the cutting. There, were the stars above them.

"Do you see it?" I asked him, taking particular note of his face. His eyes were prominent and strained; but not very much more so, perhaps, than my own had been when I had directed them earnestly towards the same spot.

"No," he answered. "It is not there."

"Agreed," said I.

We went in again, shut the door, and resumed our seats. I was thinking how best to improve this advantage, if it might be called one, when he took up the conversation in such a matter-of-course way, so assuming that there could be no serious question of fact between us, that I felt myself placed in the weakest of positions.

"By this time you will fully understand, sir," he said, "that what troubles me so dreadfully is the question, What does the spectre mean?"

I was not sure, I told him, that I did fully understand.

"What is its warning against?" he said, ruminating, with his eyes on the fire, and only by times turning them on me. "What is the danger? Where is the danger? There is danger overhanging, somewhere on the Line. Some dreadful calamity will happen. It is not to be doubted this third time, after what has gone before. But surely this is a cruel haunting of *me*. What can *I* do?"

He pulled out his handkerchief and wiped the drops from his heated forehead.

"If I telegraph Danger on either side of me, or on both, I can give no reason for it," he went on, wiping the palms of his hands. "I should get into trouble and do no good. They would think I was mad. This is the way it would work: Message, 'Danger! Take care!' Answer, 'What danger? Where?' Message, 'Don't know. But for God's sake take care!' They would displace me. What else could they do?"

His pain of mind was most pitiable to see. It was the mental torture of a conscientious man, oppressed beyond endurance by an unintelligible responsibility involving life.

"When it first stood under the Danger-light," he went on, putting his dark hair back from his head and drawing his hands outward across and across his temples in an extremity of feverish distress, "why not tell me where that accident was to happen—if it must happen? Why not tell me how it could be averted—if it could have been averted? When on its second coming it hid its face, why not tell me instead: 'She is going to die. Let them keep her at home'? If it came, on those two occasions, only to show me that its warnings were true and so to prepare me for the third, why not warn me plainly now? And I, Lord help me! A mere poor signalman on this solitary station! Why not go to somebody with credit to be believed and power to act!"

When I saw him in this state, I saw that for the poor man's sake, as well as for the public safety, what I had to do for the time was to compose his mind. Therefore, setting aside all question of reality or unreality between us, I represented to him that whoever thoroughly discharged his duty, must do well, and that at least it was his comfort that he understood his duty, though he did not understand these confounding Appearances. In this effort I succeeded far better than in the attempt to reason him out of his conviction. He became calm; the occupations incidental to his post as the night advanced began to make larger demands on his attention; and I left him at two in the morning. I had offered to stay through the night, but he would not hear of it.

That I more than once looked back at the red light as I ascended the pathway, that I did not like the red light, and that I should have slept but poorly if my bed had been under it, I see no reason to conceal. Nor did I like the two sequences of the accident and the dead girl. I see no reason to conceal that, either.

But what ran most in my thoughts was the consideration how ought I to act, having become the recipient of this disclosure? I had proved the man to be intelligent, vigilant, painstaking, and exact; but how long might he remain so, in his state of mind? Though in a subordinate position, still he held a most important trust, and would I (for instance) like to stake my own life on the chances of his continuing to execute it with precision?

Unable to overcome a feeling that there would be something treacherous in my communicating what he had told me to his superiors in the Company, without first being plain with himself and proposing a middle course to him, I ultimately resolved to offer to accompany him (otherwise keeping his secret for the present) to the wisest medical practitioner we could hear of in those parts and to take his opinion. A change in his time of duty would come round next night, he had apprised me, and he would be off an hour or two after sunrise, and on again soon after sunset. I had appointed to return accordingly.

Next evening was a lovely evening, and I walked out early to enjoy it. The sun was not yet quite down when I traversed the field-path near the top of the deep cutting. I would extend my walk for an hour, I said to myself, half an hour on and half an hour back, and it would then be time to go to my signalman's box.

Before pursuing my stroll, I stepped to the brink and mechanically looked down from the point from which I had first seen him. I cannot describe the thrill that seized upon me when, close at the mouth of the tunnel, I saw the appearance of a man, with his left sleeve across his eyes, passionately waving his right arm.

The nameless horror that oppressed me, passed in a moment, for in a moment I saw that this appearance of a man was a man indeed, and that there was a little group of other men standing at a short distance, to whom he seemed to be rehearsing the gesture he made. The Danger-light was not yet lighted. Against its shaft a little low hut, entirely new to me, had been made of some wooden supports and tarpaulin. It looked no bigger than a bed.

With an irresistible sense that something was wrong—with a flashing self-reproachful fear that fatal mischief had come of my leaving the man there, and causing no one to be sent to overlook or correct what he did—I descended the notched path with all the speed I could make.

"What is the matter?" I asked the men.

"Signalman killed this morning, sir."

"Not the man belonging to that box?"

"Yes, sir."

"Not the man I know?"

"You will recognise him, sir, if you knew him," said the man who spoke for the others, solemnly uncovering his own head and raising an end of the tarpaulin, "for his face is quite composed."

"O! how did this happen, how did this happen?" I asked, turning from one to another as the hut closed in again.

"He was cut down by an engine, sir. No man in England knew his work better. But somehow he was not clear of the outer rail. It was just at broad day. He had struck the light and had the lamp in his hand. As the engine came out of the tunnel his back was towards her, and she cut him down. That man drove her, and was showing how it happened. Show the gentleman, Tom."

The man, who wore a rough dark dress, stepped back to his former place at the mouth of the tunnel.

"Coming round the curve in the tunnel, sir," he said, "I saw him at the end, like as if I saw him down a perspective-glass. There was no time to check speed, and I knew him to be very careful. As he didn't seem to take heed of the whistle, I shut it off when we were running down upon him, and called to him as loud as I could call."

"What did you say?"

"I said 'Below there! Look out! Look out! For God's sake clear the way!'"

I started.

"Ah! it was a dreadful time, sir. I never left off calling to him. I put this arm before my eyes, not to see, and I waved this arm to the last; but it was no use."

Without prolonging the narrative to dwell on any one of its curious circumstances more than on any other, I may, in closing it, point out the coincidence that the warning of the engine-driver included not only the words which the unfortunate signalman had repeated to me as haunting him but also the words which I myself—not he—had attached, and that only in my own mind, to the gesticulation he had imitated.

Katherine Mansfield

Katherine Mansfield was born in 1888 in Wellington, New Zealand. Between 1903 and 1906 she was a student at Queen's College, London. On her return home she rebelled against the provinciality of New Zealand and resented the prim criticism that greeted her early literary efforts. After some bitter arguments with her family, she left again for London in 1908. A skilful performer on the violoncello, she could not decide at first whether to follow a musical or a literary career. Her marriage, which she embarked upon in 1909, much against her father's wishes, soon broke up and she moved to Germany. The following period of unhappiness resulted in her first book, a series of bitter sketches entitled *In a German Pension*, published in 1911.

Returning to London, she contributed stories to various periodicals, including *Rhythm*, which was edited by the well-known critic John Middleton Murray, whom she married in 1918 when her first husband finally divorced her. The horrors of the First World War, the death of her brother in 1915 and the growing mechanisation of society, had a profound effect on her writing. Her thoughts turned back to the simpler life of her childhood and many of the stories she wrote subsequently had New Zealand settings. Two of her best collections are *Bliss* and *The Garden Party*. She developed tuberculosis in 1917 and from then on led a wandering life in search of health. She was finally forced to stop writing in 1922 and died the following year at Fontainebleau in France.

THE DOLL'S HOUSE is typical of much of her work in that it provides a sensitive description of everyday events and feelings in the lives of men, women and, especially in this case, children.

The Doll's House

by Katherine Mansfield

When dear old Mrs. Hay went back to town after staying with the Burnells she sent the children a doll's house. It was so big that the carter and Pat carried it into the courtyard, and there it stayed, propped up on two wooden boxes beside the feed-room door.

There stood the doll's house, a dark oily, spinach green, picked out with bright yellow. Its two solid little chimneys, glued to the roof, were painted red and white, and the door, gleaming with yellow varnish, was like a little slab of toffee. Four windows, real windows, were divided into panes by a broad streak of green. There was actually a tiny porch, too, painted yellow, with big lumps of congealed paint hanging along the edge.

But perfect, perfect little house! Who could possibly mind the smell. It was part of the joy, part of the newness.

"Open it quickly, someone!"

The hook at the side was stuck fast. Pat prised it open with his penknife, and the whole house front swung back, and—there you were, gazing at one and the same moment into drawing-room and dining-room, the kitchen and two bedrooms.

"Oh-oh!" The Burnell children sounded as though they were in despair. It was too marvellous; it was too much for them. They had never seen anything like it in their lives. All the rooms were papered. There were pictures on the walls, painted on the paper, with gold frames complete. Red carpets covered all the floors except the kitchen; red plush chairs in the drawing-room, green in the dining-room; tables, beds with real bedclothes, a cradle, stove, a dresser with tiny plates and one big jug. But what Kezia liked more than anything, what she liked frightfully, was the lamp. It stood in the middle of the dining-room table, an exquisite little amber lamp with a white globe. It was even filled already for lighting, though, of course, you couldn't light it. But there was something inside that looked like oil and moved when you shook it. The lamp was perfect. It seemed to smile at Kezia, and say, "I live here." The lamp was real.

The Burnell children could hardly walk to school fast enough the next morning. They burned to tell everybody, to describe, to—well—to boast about their doll's house before the school-bell rang.

"I'm to tell," said Isabel, "because I'm the eldest. And you two can join in after. But I'm to tell first."

Playtime came and Isabel was surrounded. The girls of her class nearly fought to put their arms around her, to walk away with her, to beam flatteringly, to be her special friend. She held quite a court under the huge pine trees at the side of the playground. Nudging, giggling together, the little girls pressed up close. And the only two who stayed outside the ring were the two who were always outside, the little Kelveys. They knew better than to come anywhere near the Burnells.

They were the daughters of a spry, hard-working little washer-woman, who went about from house to house by the day. This was awful enough. But where was Mr. Kelvey? Nobody knew for certain. But everybody said he was in prison. So they were the daughters of a washerwoman and a gaolbird. Very nice company for other people's children! And they looked it. Why Mrs. Kelvey made them so conspicuous was hard to understand. The truth was they were dressed in "bits" given to her by the people for whom she worked. Lil, for instance, who was a stout, plain child with big freckles, came to school in a dress made from a green art-serge table-cloth of the Burnells', with red plush sleeves from the Logans' curtains. Her hat, perched on top of her high forehead, was a grown-up woman's hat, once the property of Miss Lecky, the postmistress. It was turned up at the back and trimmed with a large scarlet quill. What a little guy she looked! It was impossible not to laugh. And her little sister, our Else, wore a long white dress, rather like a nightgown, and a pair of little boy's boots. But

whatever our Else wore she would have looked strange. She was a tiny wishbone of a child, with cropped hair and enormous solemn eyes—a little white owl. Nobody had ever seen her smile; she scarcely ever spoke. She went through life holding on to Lil, with a piece of Lil's skirt screwed up in her hand. Where Lil went, our Else followed. In the playground, on the road going to and from school there was Lil marching in front and our Else holding on behind. Only when she wanted anything, or she was out of breath, our Else gave Lil a tug, a twitch, and Lil stopped and turned round. The Kelveys never failed to understand each other.

Now they hovered at the edge; you couldn't stop them listening. When the little girls turned round and sneered, Lil, as usual, gave her silly, shamefaced smile, but our Else only looked.

And Isabel's voice, so very proud, went on telling. The carpet made a great sensation, but so did the beds, with real bedclothes, and the stove with an oven door.

When she had finished Kezia broke in, "You've forgotten the lamp, Isabel."

"Oh yes," said Isabel, "and there's a teeny little lamp, all made of yellow glass with a white globe that stands on the dining-room table. You couldn't tell it from a real one."

"The lamp's best of all," cried Kezia. She thought Isabel wasn't making half enough of the little lamp. But nobody paid any attention. Isabel was choosing the two who were to come back with them that afternoon and see it. She chose Emmie Cole and Lena Logan.

Days passed, and as more children saw the doll's house, the fame of it spread.

At last everybody had seen it except the Kelveys. On that day the subject rather flagged. It was the dinner hour. The children stood together under the pine trees, and suddenly, as they looked at the Kelveys, always by themselves, always listening, they wanted to be horrid to them.

Suddenly Lena Logan gave a little squeal and danced in front of the other girls. "Watch! Watch me! Watch me now!" said Lena. And sliding, gliding, dragging one foot, giggling behind her hand, Lena went over to the Kelveys.

Lil looked up from her dinner. She wrapped the rest quickly away. Our Else stopped chewing. What was coming now?

"Is it true you're going to be a servant when you grow up, Lil Kelvey?" shrilled Lena.

Dead silence. But instead of answering, Lil only gave her silly, shamefaced smile. She didn't seem to mind the question at all. What a sell for Lena! The girls began to titter.

Lena couldn't stand that. She put her hands on her hips; she shot forward, "Yah, yer father's in prison!" she hissed spitefully.

This was such a marvellous thing to have said that the little girls rushed away in a body, deeply, deeply excited, wild with joy.

Someone found a long rope, and they began skipping. And never did they skip so high, run in and out so fast, or do such daring things as on that morning.

In the afternoon Pat called for the Burnell children with the buggy and they drove home. There were visitors. Isabel and Lottie, who liked visitors, went upstairs to change their pinafores. But Kezia thieved out at the back. Nobody was about; she began to swing on the big white gates of the courtyard. Presently, looking along the road, she saw two little dots. They grew bigger, they were coming towards her. Now she could see that there was one in front and one close behind. Now she could see that they were the Kelveys. Kezia stopped swinging. She slipped off the gate as if she were going to run away. Then she hesitated; the Kelveys came nearer, and beside them walked their shadows, very long, stretching right across the road with their heads in the buttercups. Kezia clambered back on the gate; she had made up her mind. She swung out.

"Hullo," she said to the passing Kelveys.

They were so astounded that they stopped. Lil gave her silly smile. Our Else stared.

"You can come and see our doll's house if you want to," said Kezia, and she dragged one toe on the ground. But at that Lil turned red and shook her head quickly.

"Why not?" asked Kezia.

Lil gasped, then she said, "Your ma told our ma you wasn't to speak to us."

"Oh, well," said Kezia. She didn't know what to reply. "It doesn't matter. You can come and see our doll's house all the same. Come on. Nobody's looking."

But Lil shook her head still harder.

"Don't you want to?" asked Kezia.

Suddenly there was a twitch, a tug at Lil's skirt. She turned round. Our Else was looking at her with big, imploring eyes; she was frowning; she wanted to go. For a moment Lil looked at our Else very thoughtfully. But then our Else twitched her skirt again. She started forward. Kezia led the way. Like two little stray cats they followed across the courtyard to where the doll's house stood.

"There it is," said Kezia.

There was a pause. Lil breathed loudly, almost snorted; our Else was still as stone.

"I'll open it for you," said Kezia kindly. She undid the hook and they looked inside.

"There's the drawing-room and the dining-room, and that's the—"

"Kezia!"

Oh, what a start they gave!

"Kezia!"

It was Aunt Beryl's voice. They turned round. At the back door stood Aunt Beryl, staring as if she couldn't believe what she saw.

"How dare you ask the little Kelveys into the courtyard!" said her cold, furious voice. "You know as well as I do, you're not allowed to talk to them. Run away, children, run away at once.

And don't come back again," said Aunt Beryl. And she stepped into the yard and shooed them out as if they were chickens.

"Off you go immediately!" she called, cold and proud.

They did not need telling twice. Burning with shame, shrinking together, Lil huddling along her like mother, our Else dazed, somehow they crossed the big courtyard and squeezed through the white gate.

"Wicked, disobedient little girl!" said Aunt Beryl bitterly to Kezia, and she slammed the doll's house to.

When the Kelveys were well out of sight of Burnells', they sat down to rest on a big red drainpipe by the side of the road. Lil's cheeks were still burning; she took off the hat with the quill and held it on her knee. Dreamily they looked over the hay paddocks, past the creek, to the group of wattles where Logan's cows stood waiting to be milked.

Presently our Else nudged up close to her sister. But now she had forgotten the cross lady. She put out a finger and stroked her sister's quill; she smiled her rare smile.

"I seen the little lamp," she said softly.

Then both were silent once more.

William Golding

William Golding was born in 1911 in Cornwall and was educated at Marlborough Grammar School and Brasenose College, Oxford. After serving in the Royal Navy during the Second World War, he became a schoolmaster. His keen understanding of children's thoughts, feelings and behaviour is clearly demonstrated in BILLY THE KID and in his first novel, *Lord of the Flies*, published in 1954.

Although it can be enjoyed simply as an adventure yarn about a gang of schoolboys stranded on a desert island, *Lord of the Flies* is really concerned with much more than this. Its theme is that our primitive instincts are still very strong and that if the props of civilisation—law, religion, scientific aids and so on—are removed, we quickly revert to savagery. Thus, the boys, "whose voices had been the song of angels", first become "hunters", then "savages", and lastly "devils". You may find it interesting to compare this novel with R. M. Ballantyne's *Coral Island*, the nineteenth-century classic in which right always triumphs over evil.

Another of William Golding's novels which can be enjoyed for its story alone, but which is primarily concerned with the question of evil in Man's evolution, is *The Inheritors*. Lok and his family are ape-men who are gradually exterminated by the "true" men of the Stone Age. Most of the events are seen through the eyes of Lok, who thinks not in words but in pictures. Near the end of the book, however, we enter the more calculating mind of Tuami, one of the invaders.

Unless you find that these two novels present no difficulties, it may be advisable to leave Golding's other, more complex, stories until a later stage in your reading.

Billy the Kid

by William Golding

On the first day, Lily, my nurse, took me to school. We went hand-in-hand through the churchyard, down the Town Hall steps, and along the south side of the High Street. The school was at the bottom of an alley; two rooms, one downstairs and one upstairs, a staircase, a place for hanging coats, and a lavatory. "Miss" kept the school—handsome, good-tempered Miss, who I liked so much. Miss used the lower room for prayers and singing and drill and meetings, and the upper one for all the rest. Lily hung my coat up, took me upstairs, and deposited me among a score or so of children who ranged in age from five to eleven. The boys were neatly dressed, and the girls over-dressed if anything. Miss taught in the old-fashioned way, catering for all ages at once.

I was difficult.

No one had suggested, before this time, that anything mattered outside myself. I was used to being adored, for I was an attractive child. Indeed, my mother would declare that I had "eyes like cornflowers and hair like a field of ripe corn". I had known no one outside my own family—nothing but walks with Lily or my parents and long holidays by a Cornish sea. I had read much for my age but saw no point in figures. I had a passion for words in themselves, and collected them like stamps or birds' eggs.

I had also a clear picture of what school was to bring me. It was to bring me fights. I lacked opposition, and yearned to be victorious.

It did not occur to me that school might have discipline or that numbers might be necessary. While, therefore, I was supposed to be writing out my tables, or even dividing four oranges between two poor boys, I was more likely to be scrawling a list of words, butt (barrel), butter, butt (see goat). While I was supposed to be learning my Collect, I was likely to be chanting inside my head a list of delightful words which I had picked up—deebriss and skirmishar, creskent and sweeside. On this first day, when Miss taxed me with my apparent inactivity, I smiled and said nothing until she went away.

I had quickly narrowed my interest in school to the quarter of an hour between eleven and fifteen minutes past. This was Break, when our society at last lived up to my expectations. While Miss sat at her desk and drank tea, we spent the Break playing and fighting in the space between the desks and the door. The noise rose slowly in shrillness and intensity, so that I could soon assess the exact note at which Miss would ring a handbell and send us back to our books. If we were dull and listless, Break might be extended by as much as ten minutes; so there was a constant conflict in my mind—a desire to be rowdy, and a leader in rowdiness, together with the knowledge that success would send us back to our desks.

The games were numerous and varied with our sex. The girls played with dolls or at weddings. Most of the time they played Postman's Knock among themselves—played it seriously, like a kind of innocent apprenticeship.

> Tap! Tap!
> "Who's there?"
> "A letter for Mary."

We boys ignored them with a contempt of inexpressible depth. We did not kiss each other, not we. We played tag or fought in knots and clusters.

Fighting proved to be just as delightful as I had thought. I was chunky and zestful and enjoyed hurting people. I exulted in victory, in the complete subjugation of my adversary, and thought that they should enjoy it, too—or at least be glad to suffer for my sake. For this reason, I was puzzled when the supply of opponents diminished. Soon I had to corner victims before I could get a fight at all.

There were whisperings in corners and on the stairs. There were meetings. There were conversations which ceased when I came near. Suddenly in Break, when I tried to fight, the opposition fled with screams of hysterical laughter, then combined in democratic strength and hurled itself on my back. As for the little girls, they no longer played Postman's Knock, but danced on the skirts of the scrum, and screamed encouragement to the just majority.

That Break ended early. When we were back at our desks, I found my rubber was gone, and no one would lend me another. But I needed a rubber, so I chewed up a piece of paper and used that. Miss detected my fault and cried out in mixed horror and amusement. Now the stigma of dirt was added to the others.

At the end of the morning I was left disconsolate in my desk. The other boys and girls clamoured out purposefully. I wandered after them, puzzled at a changing world. But they had not gone far. They were grouped on the cobbles of the alley, outside the door. The boys stood warily in a semicircle, their satchels swinging loose. The girls were ranged behind them, ready to send their men into the firing line. The girls were excited and giggling, but the boys were pale and grim.

"Go on!" shouted the girls, "Go on!"

The boys took cautious steps forward.

Now I saw what was to happen—felt shame, and the bitterness of all my seven beings. Humiliation gave me strength. A rolled-up exercise book became an epic sword. I went mad. With what felt like a roar, but must really have been a pig-squeal, I leapt at the nearest boy and hit him squarely on the nose. Then I was round the semi-circle, hewing and thumping. The screams of the little girls went needle sharp. A second or two later, they and the boys were broken and running up the alley, piling through the narrow entry, erupting into the street.

I stood alone on the cobbles and a wave of passionate sorrow engulfed me. Indignation and affront, shame and frustration took command of my muscles and my lungs. My voice rose in a sustained howl, for all the world as though I had been the loser. I began to zigzag up the alley, head back, my voice serenading a vast sorrow in the sky. My feet found their way along the High Street, and my sorrow went before me like a brass band. Past the Antique Shoppe, the International Stores, Barclay's Bank; past

the tobacconist's and the Green Dragon, with head back, and grief as shrill and steady as a siren. . . .

I suspected that my reservoirs were not sufficient for the waters of lamentation, suspected that my voice would disappear, and that I was incapable of a half-mile's sustained emotion. I began to run, therefore, so that my sorrow would last. When suspicion turned to certainty, I cut my crying to a whimper and settled to the business of getting it home. Past the Aylesbury Arms, across the London Road, through Oxford Street by the Wesleyan Chapel, turn left for the last climb in the Green—and there my feeling inflated like a balloon, so that I did the last twenty yards as tragically as I could have wished, swimming through an ocean of sorrow, all quite genuine—swung on the front-door knob, stumbled in, staggered to my mother . . .

"Why, Billy! Whatever's the matter?"

. . . balloon burst, floods, tempests, hurricanes, rage and anguish—a monstrous yell . . .

"THEY DON'T LIKE ME!"

102

My mother administered consolation and the hesitant suggestion that perhaps some of the transaction had been my fault. But I was beyond the reach of such footling ideas. She comforted, my father and Lily hovered, until at last I was quiet enough to eat. My mother put on her enormous hat and went out with an expression of grim purpose. When she came back, she said she thought everything would be all right. I continued to eat and sniff and hiccup. I brooded righteously on what was going to happen to my schoolfellows now that my mother had taken a hand. They were, I thought, probably being sent to bed without anything to eat, and it would serve them right and teach them to like me and not be cruel. After lunch, I enjoyed myself darkly inventing possible punishments for them—lovely punishments.

Miss called later and had a long talk with my mother in the drawing-room. As she left, I stuck my field of ripe corn round the dining-room door again and saw them.

"Bring him along a quarter of an hour late," said Miss. "That's all I shall need."

Next day at school everyone was seated and you could have stuck a fork into the air of noiseless excitement. Wherever I looked there were faces that smiled shyly at me. I inspected them for signs of damage but no one seemed to have suffered any crippling torment. I reached for a rubber, and a girl in pink and plaits leaned over.

"Borrow mine."

A boy offered me a handkerchief. Another passed me a note with "wil you jine me ggang" written on it. I was in. We began to say our tables and I only had to pause for breath before giving an answer to six sevens for a gale of whispers to suggest sums varying from thirty-nine to forty-five. Dear Miss had done her work well, and today I should enjoy hearing her fifteen minutes' sermon on brotherly love. Indeed, school seemed likely to come to a full stop from sheer excess of charity; so Miss, smiling remotely, said we would have an extra long Break. My heart leapt, because I thought that now we could get on with some really fierce, friendly fighting, with even a bloody nose. But Miss produced a train set. When the other boys got down to fixing rails, the girls, inexpressibly moved by the sermon, seized me in posse. I never

stood a chance against those excited arms, those tough, silken chests, those bird-whistling mouths, that mass of satin and serge and wool and pigtails and ribbons. Before I knew where I was, I found myself, my cornflower eyes popping out of my head, playing Postman's Knock.

The first girl to go outside set the pattern.

"A parcel for Billy Golding!"

In and out I went like a weaver's shuttle, pecked, pushed, hugged, mouthed and mauled, in and out from fair to dark to red, from Eunice who had had fever and a crop, to big Martha who could sit on her hair.

I kissed the lot.

This was, I suppose, my first lesson; and I cannot think it was successful. For I did not know about the sermon then. I merely felt that the boys and girls who tried to do democratic justice on me had been shown to be wrong. I was, and now they knew it, a thoroughly likeable character. I was unique and precious after all; and I still wondered what punishments their parents had found for them which had forced them to realise the truth.

I still refused to do my lessons, confronting Miss with an impenetrable placidity. I still enjoyed fighting if I was given the chance. I still had no suspicion that Billy was anything but perfect. At the end of term, when I went down to Cornwall, I sat in a crowded carriage with my prize book open on my knees for six hours, so that passengers could read the inscription. I am reading it now:

Billy Golding

1919

Prize for

General Improvement

Edna O'Brien

Edna O'Brien was born in 1932 in Tuamgraney, County Clare. She attended pharmaceutical college in Dublin, but practised pharmacy for only a short time. Her first novel, *The Country Girls*, was published in 1960. Since then she has been a full-time writer and has produced a number of other novels, a collection of short stories (*The Love Object*), a stage play and several screenplays including *The Girl with Green Eyes* and *Three into Two Won't Go*.

Although she is widely recognised as one of the most talented of contemporary writers, many of her books are banned in her own country. This is partly because of the direct way in which she sometimes writes about sexual relationships. She is not concerned, as many women writers have been, with false romance and happy endings but with women's real feelings and thoughts. This, however, is only one aspect of her work. She also explores other attitudes that separate men and women, the hypocrisy of the Establishment and the harshness of life in a poor country. Although a note of despair runs through much of her work, it is often balanced by her comic inventiveness.

You may find it difficult to identify with some of the characters and settings in her stories but they are worth pursuing. *The Country Girls* is probably the most suitable book to start with. Like THE RUG, it is a vivid reconstruction of the delights and disappointments of an Irish country childhood.

Of her approach to writing she has said: "My aim is to write books that in some way celebrate life and do justice to my emotions as well as form a connection with the reader."

The Rug

by Edna O'Brien

I went down on my knees upon the brand-new linoleum, and smelled the strange smell. It was rich and oily. It first entered and attached itself to something in my memory when I was nine years old. I've since learned that it is the smell of linseed oil, but coming on it unexpectedly can make me both a little disturbed and sad.

I grew up in the west of Ireland, in a grey cut-stone farmhouse, which my father inherited from his father. My father came from lowland, better-off farming people, my mother from the windswept hungry hills above a great lake. As children, we played in a small forest of rhododendrons—thickened and tangled and broken under scratching cows—around the house and down the drive. The avenue up from the front gates had such great pot-holes that cars had to lurch off into the field and out again.

But though all outside was neglect, overgrown with ragwort and thistle, strangers were surprised when they entered the house; my father might fritter his life away watching the slates slip from the outhouse roofs—but, within, that safe, square, lowland house of stone was my mother's pride and joy. It was always spotless. It was stuffed with things—furniture, china dogs, Toby mugs, tall jugs, trays, tapestries and whatnots. Each of the four bedrooms had holy pictures on the walls and a gold overmantel surmounting each fireplace. In the fireplaces there were paper fans or lids of chocolate boxes. Mantelpieces carried their own close-packed array of wax flowers, holy statues, broken alarm clocks, shells, photographs, soft rounded cushions for sticking pins in.

My father was generous, foolish, and so idle that it could only have been some sort of illness. That year in which I was nine and first experienced the wonderful smell, he sold another of the meadows to pay off some debt, and for the first time in many years my mother got a lump of money.

She went out early one morning and caught the bus to the city, and through a summer morning and afternoon she trudged around looking at linoleums. When she came home in the evening, her feet hurting from high heels, she said she had bought some beautiful light-brown linoleum, with orange squares on it.

The day came when the four rolls were delivered to the front gates, and Hickey, our farm help, got the horse and cart ready to bring it up. We all went; we were that excited. The calves followed the cart, thinking that maybe they were to be fed down by the roadside. At times they galloped away but came back again, each calf nudging the other out of the way. It was a warm, still day, the sounds of cars and neighbours' dogs carried very distinctly and the cow lats on the drive were brown and dry like flake tobacco.

My mother did most of the heaving and shoving to get the rolls on to the cart. She had early accepted that she had been born to do the work.

She may have bribed Hickey with the promise of hens to sell for himself, because that evening he stayed in to help with the floor—he usually went over to the village and drank a pint or two of stout. Mama, of course, always saved newspapers, and she said that the more we laid down under the lino the longer it would wear. On her hands and knees, she looked up once—flushed, delighted, tired—and said, "Mark my words, we'll see a carpet in here yet."

There was calculation and argument before cutting the difficult bits around the door frames, the bay window, and the fireplace. Hickey said that without him my mother would have botched the whole thing. In the quick flow of argument and talk, they did not notice that it was past my bedtime. My father sat outside in the kitchen by the stove all evening while we worked. Later, he came in and said what a grand job we were doing. A grand job, he said. He'd had a headache.

The next day must have been Saturday, for I sat in the sitting-room all morning admiring the linoleum, smelling its smell, counting the orange squares. I was supposed to be dusting. Now and then I re-arranged the blinds, as the sun moved. We had to keep the sun from fading the bright colours.

The dogs barked and the postman cycled up. I ran out and met him carrying a huge parcel. Mama was away up in the yard with the hens. When the postman had gone, I went up to tell her.

"A parcel?" she said. She was cleaning the hens' trough before putting their food in it. The hens were moiling around, falling in and out of the buckets, pecking at her hands. "It's just binding twine for the baling machine," she said. "Who'd be sending parcels?" She was never one to lose her head.

I said that the parcel had a Dublin postmark—the postman told me that—and that there was some black woolly thing in it. The paper was torn at the corner, and I'd pushed a finger in, fearfully.

Coming down to the house she wiped her hands with a wad of long grass. "Perhaps somebody in America has remembered us at last." One of her few dreams was to be remembered by relatives who had gone to America. The farm buildings were some way from the house; we ran the last bit. But, even in her excitement, her careful nature forced her to unknot every length of string from the parcel and roll it up, for future use. She was the world's most generous woman, but was thrifty about saving twine and paper, and candle stumps, and turkey wings and empty pill boxes.

"My God," she said reverently, folding back the last piece of paper and revealing a black sheepskin hearth-rug. We opened it out. It was a half-moon shape and covered the kitchen table. She could not speak. It was real sheepskin, thick and soft and luxurious. She examined the lining, studied the maker's label in the back, searched through the folds of brown paper for a possible letter, but there was nothing at all to indicate where it had come from.

"Get me my glasses," she said. We read the address again, and the postmark. The parcel had been sent from Dublin two days before. "Call your father," she said. He was in bed with rheumatic pains. Rug or no rug, he demanded a fourth cup of tea before he could get up.

We carried the big black rug into the sitting-room and laid it down upon the new linoleum, before the fireplace.

"Isn't it perfect, a perfect colour scheme?" she said. The room had suddenly become cosy. She stood back and looked at it with surprise, and a touch of suspicion. Though she was always hoping, she never really expected things to turn out well. At nine years old, I knew enough about my mother's life to say a prayer of thanks that at last she had got something she wanted, and without having to work for it. She had a round, sallow face and a peculiarly uncertain, timid smile. The suspicion soon left her, and the smile came out. That was one of her happiest days; I remember it as I remember her unhappiest day to my knowledge—the day the bailiff came, a year later. I hoped she would sit in the newly-appointed room on Sundays for tea, without her apron, with her brown hair combed out, looking calm and beautiful. Outside, the rhododendrons, though wild and broken, would bloom red and purple and, inside, the new rug would lie upon the richly smelling linoleum. She hugged me suddenly, as if I were the one to thank for it all; the hen mash had dried on her hands and they had the mealy smell I knew so well.

For spells during the next few days, my mother racked her brain, and she racked our brains, for a clue. It had to be someone who knew something of her needs and wants—how else could he have decided upon just the thing she needed? She wrote letters here and there, to distant relations, to friends, to people she had not seen for years.

"Must be one of *your* friends," she would say to my father.

"Oh, probably, probably. I've known a lot of decent people in my time."

She was referring—ironically, of course—to the many strangers to whom he had offered tea. He liked nothing better than to stand down at the gates on a fair day or a race day, engaging passers-by in conversation and finally bringing someone up to the house for tea and boiled eggs. He had a genius for making friends.

"I'd say that's it," my father said, delighted to take credit for the rug.

In the warm evenings we sat around the fireplace—we'd never had a fire in that room throughout the whole of my childhood—and around the rug, listening to the radio. And now and then, Mama or Dada would remember someone else from whom the rug might have come. Before a week had passed, she had written to a dozen people—an acquaintance who had moved up to Dublin with a greyhound pup Dada had given him, which greyhound had turned out a winner; an unfrocked priest who had stayed in our house for a week, gathering strength from Mama to travel on home and meet his family; a magician who had stolen Dada's gold watch and never been seen since; a farmer who once sold us a tubercular cow and would not take it back.

Weeks passed. The rug was taken out on Saturdays and shaken well, the new lino polished. Once, coming home early from school, I looked in the window and saw Mama kneeling on the rug saying a prayer. I'd never seen her pray like that, in the middle of the day, before. My father was going into the next county the following day to look at a horse he thought he might get cheap; she was, of course, praying that he would keep his promise and not touch a drink. If he did, he might be off on a wild progress and would not be seen for a week.

He went the next day; he was to stay overnight with relations. While he was away, I slept with Mama, for company, in the big brass bed. I wakened to see a candle flame, and Mama hurriedly putting on her cardigan. Dada had come home? No, she said, but she had been lying awake thinking, and there was something she had to tell Hickey or she would not get a wink of sleep. It was not yet twelve; he might be awake. I didn't want to be left in the dark, I said, but she was already hurrying along the landing. I nipped out of bed, and followed. The luminous clock said a quarter to twelve. From the first landing, I looked over and saw her turning the knob of Hickey's door.

Why should he open his door to her then? I thought; he never let anyone in at any time, keeping the door locked when he was out on the farm. Once we climbed in through the window and found things in such a muddle—his good suit laid out flat on the floor, a shirt soaking in a bucket of dirty green water, a milk can in which there was curdled buttermilk, a bicycle chain, a broken Sacred Heart and several pairs of worn, distorted, cast-off boots—that she resolved never to set foot in it again.

"What the hell is it?" Hickey said. Then there was a thud. He must have knocked something over while he searched for his flashlamp.

"If it's fine tomorrow, we'll cut the turf," Mama said.

Hickey asked if she'd wakened him at that hour to tell him something he already knew—they discussed it at tea-time.

"Open the door," she said. "I have a bit of news for you, about the rug."

He opened the door just a fraction. "Who sent it?" he asked.

"That party from Ballinsloe," she said.

"That party" was her phrase for her two visitors who had come to our house years before—a young girl, and an older man who wore brown gauntlet gloves. Almost as soon as they'd arrived, my father went out with them in their motor-car. When they returned to our house an hour later, I gathered from the conversation that they had been to see our local doctor, a friend of Dad's. The girl was the sister of a nun, who was headmistress at the convent where my sisters were. She had been crying. I guessed then, or maybe later, that her tears had to do with her having a baby and that Dada had taken her to the doctor so that she could find out for certain if she were pregnant and make preparations to get married. It would have been impossible for her to go to a doctor in her own neighbourhood, and I had no doubt but that Dada was glad to do a favour for the nun, as he could not always pay the fees for my sisters' education. Mama gave them tea on a tray—not a spread with hand-embroidered cloth and bone-china cups—and shook hands with them coolly when they were leaving. She could not abide sinful people.

"Nice of them to remember," Hickey said, sucking air between his teeth and making bird noises. "How did you find out?"

"I just guessed," Mama told him.

"Oh, Christ!" Hickey said, closing his door with a fearful bang and getting back into bed with such vehemence that I could hear the springs revolt.

Mama carried me up the stairs, because my feet were cold, and said that Hickey had not one ounce of manners.

Next day, when Dad came home sober, she told him the story, and that night she wrote to the nun. In due course, a letter came to us—with holy medals and scapulars enclosed for me—saying that neither the nun nor her married sister had sent a gift. I expect the girl had married the man with the gauntlet gloves.

" 'Twill be one of life's mysteries," Mama said, as she beat the rug against the pier, closed her eyes to escape the dust and reconciled herself to never knowing.

But a knock came on our back door four weeks later, when we were upstairs changing the sheets on the beds. "Run down and see who it is," she said.

It was a namesake of Dada's from the village, a man who always came to borrow something—a donkey, or a mowing machine, or even a spade.

"Is your mother in?" he asked, and I went halfway up the stairs and called her down.

"I've come for the rug," he said.

"What rug?" Mama asked. It was the nearest she ever got to lying. Her breath caught short and she blushed a little.

"I hear you have a new rug here. Well, 'tis our rug, because my wife's sister sent it to us months ago and we never got it."

"What are you talking about?" she said in a very sarcastic voice. He was a cowardly man, and it was said that he was so ineffectual he would call his wife in from the garden to pour him a cup of tea. I suppose my mother hoped that she would frighten him off.

"The rug the postman brought here one morning, and handed it to your youngster there." He nodded at me.

"Oh, that," Mama said, a little stunned by the news that the postman had given information about it. Then a ray of hope, or a ray of lunacy, must have struck her, because she asked what colour of rug he was inquiring about.

"A black sheepskin," he said.

There could be no more doubt about it. Her whole being

114

drooped—shoulders, stomach, voice, everything.

"It's here," she said absently, and she went through the hall into the sitting-room.

"Being namesakes and that, the postman got us mixed up," he said stupidly to me.

She had winked at me to stay there and see he did not follow her, because she did not want him to know that we had been using it.

It was rolled and had a piece of cord around the middle when she handed it to him. As she watched him go down the avenue she wept, not so much for the loss—though the loss was enormous—as for her own foolishness in thinking that someone had wanted to do her a kindness at last.

"We live and learn," she said, as she undid her apron strings, out of habit, and then retied them slowly and methodically, making a tighter knot.

Joseph Conrad

Joseph Conrad was born in 1857 in Poland, the only child of a wealthy Polish writer and landowner who was later exiled for his political activities. At the age of eleven he was orphaned and an uncle acted as his guardian until 1874 when, much against his uncle's wishes, he went to Marseilles to enlist as a sailor. After four years at sea, including a spell of gun-running, he joined a British freighter. He gained his Master's Certificate in 1886, the year in which he became a naturalised British subject. In 1895, after extensive service on the Eastern seas and as captain of a river steamer in the Congo, he retired from the Merchant Navy to devote himself to writing. He subsequently became recognised as a major English novelist, although he did not learn the English language until he was twenty.

"If you knew," he once said, "how much every line has cost me to get out, you would understand my anxiety that none should be lost."

Conrad's work may, at times, seem involved and rather wordy. But the tales in *A Set of Six*, from which AN ANARCHIST is taken, provide a fairly simple introduction, as do those in *Typhoon and Other Stories*. *Typhoon* is about a faithful, unimaginative seaman, Captain McWhirr, and his struggle against the menace of a typhoon and the threat of rioting coolies. The same theme—the testing of men in extreme situations—also occurs in a number of other stories, such as *Youth* and *Gaspar Ruiz*. Of his novels, *Lord Jim* is perhaps the most suitable to start with.

An Anarchist

by Joseph Conrad

That year I spent the best two months of the dry season on one of the estates—in fact, on the principal cattle estate—of a famous meat-extract manufacturing company.

B. O. S. Bos. You have seen the three magic letters on the advertisement pages of magazines and newspapers, in the windows of provision merchants, and on calendars for next year you receive by post in the month of November. They scatter pamphlets also, written in a sickly enthusiastic style and in several languages, giving statistics of slaughter and bloodshed enough to make a Turk turn faint. The "art" illustrating that "literature" represents in vivid and shining colours a large and enraged black bull stamping upon a yellow snake writhing in emerald-green grass, with a cobalt-blue sky for a background. It is atrocious and it is an allegory. The snake symbolises disease, weakness— perhaps mere hunger, which last is the chronic disease of the majority of mankind. Of course, everybody knows the B.O.S. Ltd., with its unrivalled products: Vinobos, Jellybos, and the latest unequalled perfection, Tribos, whose nourishment is offered to you not only highly concentrated, but already half digested. Such apparently is the love that Limited Company bears to its fellow-men—even as the love of the father and mother penguin for their hungry fledglings.

Of course, the capital of a country must be productively employed. I have nothing to say against the company. But being myself animated by feelings of affection towards my fellow-men, I am saddened by the modern system of advertising. Whatever

117

evidence it offers of enterprise, ingenuity, impudence and resource in certain individuals, it proves to my mind the wide prevalence of that form of mental degradation which is called gullibility.

In various parts of the civilised and uncivilised world I have had to swallow B. O. S. with more or less benefit to myself, though without great pleasure. Prepared with hot water and abundantly peppered to bring out the taste, this extract is not really unpalatable. But I have never swallowed its advertisements. Perhaps they have not gone far enough. As far as I can remember they make no promise of everlasting youth to the users of B. O. S., nor yet have they claimed the power of raising the dead for their estimable products. Why this austere reserve, I wonder! But I don't think they would have had me even on these terms. Whatever form of mental degradation I may (being but human) be suffering from, it is not the popular form. I am not gullible.

I have been at some pains to bring out distinctly this statement about myself in view of the story which follows. I have checked the facts as far as possible. I have turned up the files of French newspapers, and I have also talked with the officer who commands the military guard on the *Île Royale*, when in the course of my travels I reached Cayenne. I believe the story to be in the main true. It is the sort of story that no man, I think, would ever invent about himself, for it is neither grandiose nor flattering, nor yet funny enough to gratify a perverted vanity.

It concerns the engineer of the steam-launch belonging to the Marañon cattle estate of the B. O. S. Co., Ltd. This estate is also an island—an island as big as a small province, lying in the estuary of a great South American river. It is wild and not beautiful, but the grass growing on its low plains seems to possess exceptionally nourishing and flavouring qualities. It resounds with the lowing of innumerable herds—a deep and distressing sound under the open sky, rising like a monstrous protest of prisoners condemned to death. On the mainland, across twenty miles of discoloured muddy water, there stands a city whose name, let us say, is Horta.

But the most interesting characteristic of this island (which seems like a sort of penal settlement for condemned cattle) consists in its being the only known habitat of an extremely rare and gorgeous butterfly. The species is even more rare than it is beautiful, which is not saying little. I have already alluded to my travels. I travelled at that time, but strictly for myself and with a moderation unknown in our days of round-the-world tickets. I even travelled with a purpose. As a matter of fact, I am—"Ha, ha, ha!—a desperate butterfly-slayer. Ha, ha, ha!"

This was the tone in which Mr. Harry Gee, the manager of the cattle station, alluded to my pursuits. He seemed to consider me the greatest absurdity in the world. On the other hand, the B. O. S. Co., Ltd., represented to him the acme of the nineteenth century's achievement. I believe that he slept in his leggings and spurs. His days he spent in the saddle flying over the plains, followed by a train of half-wild horsemen, who called him Don Enrique, and who had no definite idea of the B. O. S. Co., Ltd., which paid their wages. He was an excellent manager, but I don't see why, when we met at meals, he should have thumped me on the back, with loud derisive inquiries: "How's the deadly sport today? Butterflies going strong? Ha, ha, ha!"—especially as he charged me two dollars per diem for the hospitality of the B. O. S. Co., Ltd. (capital £1,500,000, fully paid up), in whose balance-sheet for that year those monies are no doubt included. "I don't think I can make it anything less in justice to my company," he had remarked, with extreme gravity, when I was arranging with him the terms of my stay on the island.

His chaff would have been harmless enough if intimacy of intercourse in the absence of all friendly feeling were not a thing detestable in itself. Moreover, his facetiousness was not very amusing. It consisted in the wearisome repetition of descriptive phrases applied to people with a burst of laughter. "Desperate butterfly-slayer. Ha, ha, ha!" was one sample of his peculiar wit which he himself enjoyed so much. And in the same vein of exquisite humour he called my attention to the engineer of the steam-launch, one day, as we strolled on the path by the side of the creek.

The man's head and shoulders emerged above the deck, over which were scattered various tools of his trade and a few pieces of machinery. He was doing some repairs to the engines. At the sound of our footsteps he raised anxiously a grimy face with a pointed chin and a tiny fair moustache. What could be seen of his delicate features under the black smudges appeared to me wasted and livid in the greenish shade of the enormous tree spreading its foliage over the launch moored close to the bank.

To my great surprise, Harry Gee addressed him as "Crocodile", in that half-jeering, half-bullying tone which is characteristic of self-satisfaction in his delectable kind:

"How does the work get on, Crocodile!"

I should have said before that the amiable Harry had picked up French of a sort somewhere—in some colony or other—and that he pronounced it with a disagreeable, forced precision as though he meant to guy the language. The man in the launch answered him quickly in a pleasant voice. His eyes had a liquid softness and his teeth flashed dazzlingly white between his thin drooping lips. The manager turned to me, very cheerful and loud, explaining:

"I call him Crocodile because he lives half in, half out of the creek. Amphibious—see? There's nothing else amphibious living on the island except crocodiles; so he must belong to the species—eh? But in reality he's nothing less than *un citoyen anarchiste de Barcelone*."

"A citizen anarchist from Barcelona?" I repeated, stupidly, looking down at the man. He had turned to his work in the engine-well of the launch and presented his bowed back to us. In that attitude I heard him protest, very audibly:

"I do not even know Spanish."

"Hey? What? You dare to deny you come from over there?" the accomplished manager was down on him truculently.

At this the man straightened himself up, dropping a spanner he had been using, and faced us; but he trembled in all his limbs.

"I deny nothing, nothing, nothing!" he said, excitedly.

He picked up the spanner and went to work again without paying any further attention to us. After looking at him for a minute or so, we went away.

"Is he really an anarchist?" I asked, when out of earshot.

"I don't care a hang what he is," answered the humorous official of the B. O. S. Co. "I gave him the name because it suited me to label him in that way. It's good for the company."

"For the company!" I exclaimed, stopping short.

"Aha!" he triumphed, tilting up his hairless pug face and straddling his thin long legs. "That surprises you. I am bound to do my best for my company. They have enormous expenses. Why—our agent in Horta tells me they spend fifty thousand pounds every year in advertising all over the world! One can't be too economical in working the show. Well, just you listen. When I took charge here the estate had no steam-launch. I asked for one, and kept on asking by every mail till I got it; but the man they sent out with it chucked his job at the end of two months, leaving the launch moored at the pontoon in Horta. Got a better screw at a sawmill up the river—blast him! And ever since it has been the same thing. Any Scotch or Yankee vagabond that likes to call himself a mechanic out here gets eighteen pounds a month, and the next you know he's cleared out, after smashing something as likely as not. I give you my word that some of the objects I've had for engine-drivers couldn't tell the boiler from the funnel. But this fellow understands his trade, and I don't mean him to clear out. See?"

And he struck me lightly on the chest for emphasis. Disregarding his peculiarities of manner, I wanted to know what all this had to do with the man being an anarchist.

"Come!" jeered the manager. "If you saw suddenly a barefooted, unkempt chap slinking amongst the bushes on the sea face of the island, and at the same time observed less than a mile from the beach a small schooner full of niggers hauling off in a hurry, you wouldn't think the man fell there from the sky, would you? And it could be nothing else but either that or Cayenne. I've got my wits about me. Directly I sighted this queer game I said to myself: 'Escaped Convict.' I was as certain of it as I am of seeing you standing here this minute. So I spurred on straight at him. He stood his ground for a bit on a sand hillock crying out: '*Monsieur! Monsieur! Arrêtez!*' then at the last moment broke and ran for life. Says I to myself, 'I'll tame you before I'm done with you.' So without a single word I kept on, heading him off here and there. I rounded him up towards the shore, and at last I had him corralled on a spit, his heels in the water and nothing but sea and sky at his back, with my horse pawing the sand and shaking his head within a yard of him."

"He folded his arms on his breast then and stuck his chin up in a sort of desperate way; but I wasn't to be impressed by the beggar's posturing.

"Says I, 'You're a runaway convict.'

"When he heard French, his chin went down and his face changed.

" 'I deny nothing,' says he, panting yet, for I had kept him skipping about in the front of my horse pretty smartly. I asked him what he was doing there. He had got his breath by then, and explained that he had meant to make his way to a farm which he understood (from the schooner's people, I suppose) was to be found in the neighbourhood. At that I laughed aloud and he got uneasy. Had he been deceived? Was there no farm within walking distance?

"I laughed more and more. He was on foot, and of course the first bunch of cattle he came across would have stamped him to rags under their hoofs. A dismounted man caught on the feeding-grounds hasn't got the ghost of a chance.

" 'My coming upon you like this has certainly saved your life,' I said. He remarked that perhaps it was so; but that for his part he had imagined I had wanted to kill him under the hoofs of my horse. I assured him that nothing would have been easier had I meant it. And then we came to a sort of dead stop. For the life of me I didn't know what to do with this convict, unless I chucked him into the sea. It occurred to me to ask him what he had been transported for. He hung his head.

" 'What is it?' says I. 'Theft, murder, rape, or what?' I wanted to hear what he would have to say for himself, though of course I expected it would be some sort of lie. But all he said was: " 'Make it what you like. I deny nothing. It is no good denying anything.'

"I looked him over carefully and a thought struck me.

" 'They've got anarchists there, too,' I said. 'Perhaps you're one of them.'

" 'I deny nothing whatever, monsieur,' he repeats.

"This answer made me think that perhaps he was not an anarchist. I believe those damned lunatics are rather proud of themselves. If he had been one, he would have probably confessed straight out.

" 'What were you before you became a convict?'

" '*Ouvrier*,' he says. 'And a good workman, too.'

"At that I began to think he must be an anarchist, after all. That's the class they come mostly from, isn't it? I hate the cowardly bomb-throwing brutes. I almost made up my mind to turn my horse short round and leave him to starve or drown where he was, whichever he liked best. As to crossing the island to bother me again, the cattle would see to that. I don't know what induced me to ask:

" 'What sort of workman?'

"I didn't care a hang whether he answered me or not. But when he said at once, '*Mécanicien, monsieur*,' I nearly jumped out of the saddle with excitement. The launch had been lying disabled and idle in the creek for three weeks. My duty to the company was clear. He noticed my start, too, and there we were for a minute or so staring at each other as if bewitched.

124

" 'Get up on my horse behind me,' I told him. 'You shall put my steam-launch to rights.' "

These are the words in which the worthy manager of the Marañon estate related to me the coming of the supposed anarchist. He meant to keep him—out of a sense of duty to the company—and the name he had given him would prevent the fellow from obtaining employment anywhere in Horta. The vaqueros of the estate, when they went on leave, spread it all over the town. They did not know what an anarchist was, nor yet what Barcelona meant. They called him Anarchisto de Barcelona, as if it were his Christian name and surname. But the people in town had been reading in their papers about the anarchists in Europe and were very much impressed. Over the jocular addition of "de Barcelona" Mr. Harry Gee chuckled with immense satisfaction. "That breed is particularly murderous, isn't it? It makes the sawmills crowd still more afraid of having anything to do with him—see?" he exulted, candidly. "I hold him by that name better than if I had him chained up by the leg to the deck of the steam-launch.

"And mark," he added, after a pause, "he does not deny it. I am not wronging him in any way. He is a convict of some sort, anyhow."

"But I suppose you pay him some wages, don't you?" I asked.

"Wages! What does he want with money here? He gets his food from my kitchen and his clothing from the store. Of course I'll give him something at the end of the year, but you don't think I'd employ a convict and give him the same money I would give an honest man? I am looking after the interests of my company first and last."

I admitted that, for a company spending fifty thousand pounds every year in advertising, the strictest economy was obviously necessary. The manager of the Marañon Estancia grunted approvingly.

"And I'll tell you what," he continued: "if I were certain he's an anarchist and he had the cheek to ask me for money, I would give him the toe of my boot. However, let him have the benefit of the doubt. I am perfectly willing to take it that he has done nothing worse than to stick a knife into somebody—with extenuating circumstances—French fashion, don't you know. But that subversive sanguinary rot of doing away with all law and order in the world makes my blood boil. It's simply cutting the ground from under the feet of every decent, respectable, hard-working person. I tell you that the consciences of people who have them, like you or I, must be protected in some way; or else the first low scoundrel that came along would in every respect be just as good as myself. Wouldn't he now? And that's absurd!"

He glared at me. I nodded slightly and murmured that doubtless there was much subtle truth in his view.

The principal truth discoverable in the views of Paul the engineer was that a little thing may bring about the undoing of a man.

"*Il ne faut pas beaucoup pour perdre un homme,*" he said to me, thoughtfully, one evening.

I report this reflection in French, since the man was of Paris, not of Barcelona at all. At the Marañon he lived apart from the station, in a small shed with a metal roof and straw walls, which he called *mon atelier*. He had a work-bench there. They had given him several horse-blankets and a saddle—not that he ever had occasion to ride, but because no other bedding was used by the working-hands, who were all vaqueros—cattlemen. And on this horseman's gear, like a son of the plains, he used to sleep amongst the tools of his trade, in a litter of rusty scrap-iron, with a portable forge at his head, under the work-bench sustaining his grimy mosquito-net.

Now and then I would bring him a few candle ends saved from the scant supply of the manager's house. He was very thankful for these. He did not like to lie awake in the dark, he confessed. He complained that sleep fled from him. "*Le sommeil me fuit,*" he declared, with his habitual air of subdued stoicism, which made him sympathetic and touching. I made it clear to him that I did not attach undue importance to the fact of his having been a convict.

Thus it came about that one evening he was led to talk about himself. As one of the bits of candle on the edge of the bench

126

burned down to the end, he hastened to light another.

He had done his military service in a provincial garrison and returned to Paris to follow his trade. It was a well-paid one. He told me with some pride that in a short time he was earning no less than ten francs a day. He was thinking of setting up for himself by and by and of getting married.

Here he sighed deeply and paused. Then with a return to his stoical note:

"It seems I did not know enough about myself."

On his twenty-fifth birthday two of his friends in the repairing shop where he worked proposed to stand him a dinner. He was immensely touched by this attention.

"I was a steady man," he remarked, "but I am not less sociable than any other body."

The entertainment came off in a little café on the Boulevard de la Chapelle. At dinner they drank some special wine. It was excellent. Everything was excellent; and the world—in his own words—seemed a very good place to live in. He had good prospects, some little money laid by, and the affection of two excellent friends. He offered to pay for all the drinks after dinner, which was only proper on his part.

They drank more wine; they drank liqueurs, cognac, beer, then more liqueurs and more cognac. Two strangers sitting at the next table looked at him, he said, with so much friendliness, that he invited them to join the party.

He had never drunk so much in his life. His elation was extreme, and so pleasurable that whenever it flagged he hastened to order more drinks.

"It seemed to me," he said, in his quiet tone and looking on the ground in the gloomy shed full of shadows, "that I was on the point of just attaining a great and wonderful felicity. Another drink, I felt, would do it. The others were holding out well with me, glass for glass."

But an extraordinary thing happened. At something the strangers said his elation fell. Gloomy ideas—*des idées noires*—rushed into his head. All the world outside the café appeared to him as a dismal evil place where a multitude of poor

127

wretches had to work and slave to the sole end that a few individuals should ride in carriages and live riotously in palaces. He became ashamed of his happiness. The pity of mankind's cruel lot wrung his heart. In a voice choked with sorrow he tried to express these sentiments. He thinks he wept and swore in turns.

The two new acquaintances hastened to applaud his humane indignation. Yes. The amount of injustice in the world was indeed scandalous. There was only one way of dealing with the rotten state of society. Demolish the whole *sacrée boutique*. Blow up the whole iniquitous show.

Their heads hovered over the table. They whispered to him eloquently; I don't think they quite expected the result. He was extremely drunk—mad drunk. With a howl of rage he leaped suddenly upon the table. Kicking over the bottles and glasses, he yelled: "*Vive l'anarchie*! Death to the capitalists!" He yelled this again and again. All round him broken glass was falling, chairs were being swung in the air, people were taking each other by the throat. The police dashed in. He hit, bit, scratched and struggled, till something crashed down upon his head. . . .

He came to himself in a police cell, locked up on a charge of assault, seditious cries, and anarchist propaganda.

He looked at me fixedly with his liquid, shining eyes, that seemed very big in the dim light.

"That was bad. But even then I might have got off somehow, perhaps," he said slowly.

I doubt it. But whatever chance he had was done away with by a young socialist lawyer who volunteered to undertake his defence. In vain he assured him that he was no anarchist; that he was a quiet, respectable mechanic, only too anxious to work ten hours per day at his trade. He was represented at the trial as the victim of society and his drunken shoutings as the expression of infinite suffering. The young lawyer had his way to make, and this case was just what he wanted for a start. The speech for the defence was pronounced magnificent.

The poor fellow paused, swallowed, and brought out the statement:

"I got the maximum penalty applicable to a first offence."

I made an appropriate murmur. He hung his head and folded his arms.

"When they let me out of prison," he began, gently, "I made tracks, of course, for my old workshop. My *patron* had a particular liking for me before; but when he saw me he turned green with fright and showed me the door with a shaking hand."

While he stood in the street, uneasy and disconcerted, he was accosted by a middle-aged man who introduced himself as an engineer's fitter, too. "I know who you are," he said. "I have attended your trial. You are a good comrade and your ideas are sound. But the devil of it is that you won't be able to get work anywhere now. These bourgeois'll conspire to starve you. That's their way. Expect no mercy from the rich."

To be spoken to so kindly in the street had comforted him very much. His seemed to be the sort of nature needing support and sympathy. The idea of not being able to find work had knocked him over completely. If his *patron*, who knew him so well for a quiet, orderly, competent workman, would have nothing to do with him now—then surely nobody else would. That was clear.

The police keeping their eye on him would hasten to warn every employer inclined to give him a chance. He felt suddenly very helpless, alarmed, and idle; and he followed the middle-aged man to the *estaminet* round the corner where he met some other good companions. They assured him that he would not be allowed to starve, work or no work. They had drinks all round to the discomfiture of all employers of labour and to the destruction of society.

He sat biting his lower lip.

"That is, monsieur, how I became a *compagnon*," he said. The hand he passed over his forehead was trembling. "All the same, there's something wrong in a world where a man can get lost for a glass more or less."

He never looked up, though I could see he was getting excited under his dejection. He slapped the bench with his open palm.

"No!" he cried. "It was an impossible existence. Watched by the police, watched by the comrades, I did not belong to myself any more! Why, I could not even go to draw a few francs from my savings-bank without a comrade hanging about the door to see that I didn't bolt! And most of them were neither more nor less than housebreakers. The intelligent, I mean. They robbed the rich; they were only getting back their own, they said. When I had had some drink I believed them. There were also the fools and the mad. *Des exaltés—quoi*! When I was drunk I loved them. When I got more drink I was angry with the world. That was the best time. I found refuge from misery in rage. But one can't be always drunk—*n'est-ce pas, monsieur*? And when I was sober I was afraid to break away. They would have stuck me like a pig."

He folded his arms again and raised his sharp chin with a bitter smile.

"By and by they told me it was time to go to work. The work was to rob a bank. Afterwards a bomb would be thrown to wreck the place. My beginner's part would be to keep watch in a street at the back and to take care of a black bag with the bomb inside till it was wanted. After the meeting at which the affair was arranged a trusty comrade did not leave me an inch. I had not dared to protest; I was afraid of being done away with quietly in that room; only, as we were walking together, I wondered whether it would

130

not be better for me to throw myself suddenly into the Seine. But while I was turning it over in my mind we had crossed the bridge, and afterwards I had not the opportunity."

In the light of the candle end, with his sharp features, fluffy little moustache, and oval face, he looked at times delicately and gaily young, and then appeared quite old, decrepit, full of sorrow, pressing his folded arms to his breast.

As he remained silent I felt bound to ask:

"Well! And how did it end?"

"Deportation to Cayenne," he answered.

He seemed to think that somebody had given the plot away. As he was keeping watch in the back street, bag in hand, he was set upon by the police. "These imbeciles," had knocked him down without noticing what he had in his hand. He wondered how the bomb failed to explode as he fell. But it didn't explode.

"I tried to tell my story in court," he continued. "The president was amused. There were in the audience some idiots who laughed."

I expressed the hope that some of his companions had been caught, too. He shuddered slightly before he told me that there were two—Simon, called also Biscuit, the middle-aged fitter who spoke to him in the street, and a fellow of the name of Mafile, one of the sympathetic strangers who had applauded his sentiments and consoled his humanitarian sorrows when he got drunk in the café.

"Yes," he went on with an effort, "I had the advantage of their company over there on St. Joseph's Island, amongst some eighty or ninety other convicts. We were all classed as dangerous."

St. Joseph's Island is the prettiest of the *Îles de Salut*. It is rocky and green, with shallow ravines, bushes, thickets, groves of mango-trees, and many feathery palms. Six warders armed with revolvers and carbines are in charge of the convicts kept there.

An eight-oared galley keeps up the communication in the daytime, across a channel a quarter of a mile wide, with the *Île Royale*, where there is a military post. She makes the first trip at six in the morning. At four in the afternoon her service is over, and she is then hauled up into a little dock on the *Île Royale* and a sentry put over her and a few smaller boats. From that time till

131

next morning the island of St. Joseph remains cut off from the rest of the world, with the warders patrolling in turn the path from the warders' house to the convict huts, and a multitude of sharks patrolling the waters all round.

Under these circumstances the convicts planned a mutiny. Such a thing had never been known in the penitentiary's history before. But their plan was not without some possibility of success. The warders were to be taken by surprise and murdered during the night. Their arms would enable the convicts to shoot down the people in the galley as she came alongside in the morning. The galley once in their possession, other boats were to be captured, and the whole company was to row away up the coast.

At dusk the two warders on duty mustered the convicts as usual. Then they proceeded to inspect the huts to ascertain that everything was in order. In the second they entered they were set upon and absolutely smothered under the numbers of their assailants. The twilight faded rapidly. It was a new moon; and a heavy black squall gathering over the coast increased the profound darkness of the night. The convicts assembied in the open space, deliberating upon the next step to be taken, argued amongst themselves in low voices.

"You took part in all this?" I asked.

"No. I knew what was going to be done, of course. But why should I kill these warders? I had nothing against them. But I was afraid of the others. Whatever happened, I could not escape from them. I sat alone on the stump of a tree with my head in my hands, sick at heart at the thought of a freedom that could be nothing but a mockery to me. Suddenly I was startled to perceive the shape of a man on the path near by. He stood perfectly still, then his form became effaced in the night. It must have been the chief warder coming to see what had become of his two men. No one noticed him. The convicts kept on quarrelling over their plans. The leaders could not get themselves obeyed. The fierce whispering of that dark mass of men was very horrible.

"At last they divided into two parties and moved off. When they had passed me I rose, weary and hopeless. The path to the warders' house was dark and silent, but on each side the bushes rustled slightly. Presently I saw a faint thread of light before me.

The chief warder, followed by his three men, was approaching cautiously. But he had failed to close his dark lantern properly. The convicts had seen that faint gleam, too. There was an awful savage yell, a turmoil on the dark path, shots fired, blows, groans; and with the sound of smashed bushes, the shouts of the pursuers and the screams of the pursued, the man-hunt, the warder-hunt, passed by me into the interior of the island. I was alone. And I assure you, monsieur, I was indifferent to everything. After standing still for a while, I walked on along the path till I kicked something hard. I stooped and picked up a warder's revolver. I felt with my fingers that it was loaded in five chambers. In the gusts of wind I heard the convicts calling to each other far away, and then a roll of thunder would cover the soughing and rustling of the trees. Suddenly, a big light ran across my path very low along the ground. And it showed a woman's skirt with the edge of an apron.

"I knew that the person who carried it must be the wife of the head warder. They had forgotten all about her, it seems. A shot rang out in the interior of the island, and she cried out to herself as she ran. She passed on. I followed, and presently I saw her again. She was pulling at the cord of the big bell which hangs at the end of the landing-pier, with one hand, and with the other she was swinging the heavy lantern to and fro. This is the agreed signal for the *Île Royale* should assistance be required at night. The wind carried the sound away from our island and the light she swung was hidden from the shore side by the few trees that grow near the warders' house.

"I came up quite close to her from behind. She went on without stopping, without looking aside, as though she had been all alone on the island. A brave woman, monsieur. I put the revolver inside the breast of my blue blouse and waited. A flash of lightning and a clap of thunder destroyed both the sound and the light of the signal for an instant, but she never faltered, pulling at the cord and swinging the lantern as regularly as a machine. She was a comely woman of thirty—no more. I thought to myself, 'All that's no good on a night like this.' And I made up my mind that if a body of my fellow-convicts came down to the pier—which was sure to happen soon—I would shoot her through the head before I shot myself. I knew the "comrades" well. This idea of mine gave me quite an interest in life, monsieur; and at once, instead of remaining stupidly exposed on the pier, I retreated a little way and crouched behind a bush. I did not intend to let myself be pounced upon unawares and be prevented perhaps from rendering a supreme service to at least one human creature before I died myself.

"But we must believe the signal was seen, for the galley from *Île Royale* came over in an astonishingly short time. The woman kept right on till the light of her lantern flashed upon the officer in command and the bayonets of the soldiers in the boat. Then she sat down and began to cry.

"She didn't need me any more. I did not budge. Some soldiers were only in their shirt-sleeves, others without boots, just as the call to arms had found them. They passed by my bush at the double. The galley had been sent away for more; and the woman sat all alone crying at the end of the pier, with the lantern standing on the ground near her.

"Then suddenly I saw in the light at the end of the pier the red pantaloons of two more men. I was overcome with astonishment. They, too, started off at a run. Their tunics flapped unbuttoned and they were bare-headed. One of them panted out to the other, 'Straight on, straight on!'

"Where on earth did they spring from, I wondered. Slowly I walked down the short pier. I saw the woman's form shaken by sobs and heard her moaning more and more distinctly, 'Oh, my man! my poor man! my poor man!' I stole on quietly. She could neither hear nor see anything. She had thrown her apron over her head and was rocking herself to and fro in her grief. But I remarked a small boat fastened to the end of the pier.

"Those two men—they looked like *sous officiers*—must have come in it, after being too late, I suppose, for the galley. It is incredible that they should have thus broken the regulations from a sense of duty. And it was a stupid thing to do. I could not believe my eyes in the very moment I was stepping into that boat.

"I pulled along the shore slowly. A black cloud hung over the *Îles de Salut*. I heard firing, shouts. Another hunt had begun—the convict-hunt. The oars were too long to pull comfortably. I managed them with difficulty, though the boat herself was light.

But when I got round to the other side of the island the squall broke in rain and wind. I was unable to make head against it. I let the boat drift ashore and secured her.

"I knew the spot. There was a tumble-down old hovel standing near the water. Cowering in there, I heard through the noises of the wind and the falling downpour some people tearing through the bushes. They came out on the strand. Soldiers perhaps. A flash of lightning threw everything near me into violent relief. Two convicts!

"And directly an amazed voice exclaimed, 'It's a miracle'. It was the voice of Simon, otherwise Biscuit.

"And another voice growled, 'What's a miracle?'

" 'Why, there's a boat lying here!'

" 'You must be mad, Simon! But there is, after all, . . . A boat.'

"They seemed awed into complete silence. The other man was Mafile. He spoke again, cautiously.

" 'It is fastened up. There must be somebody here.'

"I spoke to them from within the hovel: 'I am here.'

"They came in then, and soon gave me to understand that the boat was theirs, not mine. 'There are two of us,' said Mafile, 'against you alone.'

"I got out into the open to keep clear of them for fear of getting a treacherous blow on the head. I could have shot them both where they stood. But I said nothing. I kept down the laughter rising in my throat. I made myself very humble and begged to be allowed to go. They consulted in low tones about my fate, while with my hand on the revolver in the bosom of my blouse I had their lives in my power. I let them live. I meant them to pull that boat. I represented to them with abject humility that I understood the management of a boat, and that, being three to pull, we could get a rest in turns. That decided them at last. It was time. A little more and I would have gone into screaming fits at the drollness of it."

At this point the excitement broke out. He jumped off the bench and gesticulated. The great shadows of his arms darting over roof and walls made the shed appear too small to contain his agitation.

"I deny nothing," he burst out. "I was elated, monsieur. I tasted a sort of felicity. But I kept very quiet. I took my turn at pulling all through the night. We made for the open sea, putting our trust in a passing ship. It was a foolhardy action. I persuaded them to it. When the sun rose the immensity of water was calm, and the Îles de Salut appeared only like dark specks from the top of each swell. I was steering then. Mafile, who was pulling bow, let out an oath and said 'We must rest.'

"The time to laugh had come at last. And I took my fill of it, I can tell you. I held my sides and rolled in my seat, they had such startled faces. 'What's got into him, the animal?' cries Mafile.

"And Simon, who was nearest to me, says over his shoulder to him, 'Devil take me if I don't think he's gone mad!'

"Then I produced the revolver. Aha! In a moment they both got the stoniest eyes you can imagine. Ha, ha! They were frightened. But they pulled. Oh, yes, they pulled all day, sometimes looking wild and sometimes looking faint. I lost nothing of it because I had to keep my eyes on them all the time, or else—crack!—they would have been on top of me in a second. I rested my revolver hand on my knee all ready and steered with the other. Their faces began to blister. Sky and sea seemed on fire round us and the sea steamed in the sun. The boat made a sizzling sound as she went through the water. Sometimes Mafile foamed at the mouth and sometimes he groaned. But he pulled. He dared not stop. His eyes became bloodshot all over, and he had bitten his lower lip to pieces. Simon was as hoarse as a crow.

" 'Comrade——' he begins.

" 'There are no comrades here. I am your *patron*.'

" '*Patron*, then,' he says, 'in the name of humanity let us rest.'

"I let them. There was a little rainwater washing about the bottom of the boat. I permitted them to snatch some of it in the hollow of their palms. But as I gave the command '*En route*' I caught them exchanging significant glances. They thought I would have to go to sleep some time! Aha! But I did not want to go to sleep. I was more awake than ever. It is they who went to sleep as they pulled, tumbling off the thwarts head over heels suddenly, one after another. I let them lie. All the stars were out. It was a quiet world. The sun rose. Another day. *Allez! En route!*

"They pulled badly. Their eyes rolled about and their tongues hung out. In the middle of the forenoon Mafile croaks out: 'Let us make a rush at him, Simon. I would just as soon be shot at once as to die of thirst, hunger, and fatigue at the oar.'

"But while he spoke he pulled; and Simon kept on pulling, too. It made me smile. Ah! They loved their life, these two, in this evil world of theirs, just as I used to love my life, too, before they spoiled it for me with their phrases. I let them go on to the point of exhaustion, and only then I pointed out at the sails of a ship on the horizon.

"Aha! You should have seen them revive and buckle to their work! For I kept them at it to pull right across that ship's path. They were changed. The sort of pity I had felt then left me. They looked more like themselves every minute. They looked at me with the glances I remembered so well. They were happy. They smiled.

" 'Well,' says Simon, 'the energy of that youngster has saved our lives. If he hadn't made us, we could never have pulled so far out into the track of ships. Comrade, I forgive you. I admire you.'

"And Mafile growls from forward: 'We owe you a famous debt of gratitude, comrade. You are cut out for a chief.'

"Comrade! Monsieur! Ah, what a good word! And they, such men as these two, had made it accursed. I looked at them. I remembered their lies, their promises, their menaces, and all my days of misery. Why could they not have left me alone after I came out of prison? I looked at them and thought that while they lived I could never be free. Never. Neither I nor others like me with warm hearts and weak heads. For I know I have not a strong head, monsieur. A black rage came upon me—the rage of extreme intoxication—but not against the injustice of society. Oh, no!

" 'I must be free!' I cried, furiously.

" '*Vive la liberté*!' yells that ruffian Mafile. '*Mort aux bourgeois* who send us to Cayenne! They shall soon know that we are free.'

"The sky, the sea, the whole horizon, seemed to turn red, blood red all round the boat. My temples were beating so loud that I wondered they did not hear. How is it that they did not? How is it that they did not understand?

"I heard Simon ask, 'Have we not pulled far enough out now?'

" 'Yes. Far enough,' I said. I was sorry for him; it was the other

I hated. He hauled in his oar with a loud sigh, and as he was raising his hand to wipe his forehead with the air of a man who has done his work, I pulled the trigger of my revolver and shot him like this off the knee, right through the heart.

"He tumbled down, with his head hanging over the side of the boat. I did not give him a second glance. The other cried out piercingly. Only one shriek of horror. Then all was still.

"He slipped off the thwart on to his knees and raised his clasped hands before his face in an attitude of supplication. 'Mercy,' he whispered, faintly. 'Mercy for me!—comrade.'

" 'Ah, comrade,' I said, in a low tone. 'Yes, comrade, of course. Well, then shout *Vive l'anarchie!*'

"He flung up his arms, his face up to the sky and his mouth wide open in a great yell of despair. *'Vive l'anarchie! Vive——'*

"He collapsed all in a heap, with a bullet through his head.

"I flung them both overboard. I threw away the revolver, too. Then I sat down quietly. I was free at last! At last. I did not even look towards the ship; I did not care; indeed, I think I must have gone to sleep, because all of a sudden there were shouts and I found the ship almost on top of me. They hauled me on board and secured the boat astern. They were all blacks, except the captain, who was a mulatto. He alone knew a few words of French. I could not find out where they were going nor who they were. They gave me something to eat every day; but I did not like the way they used to discuss me in their language. Perhaps they were deliberating about throwing me overboard in order to keep possession of the boat. How do I know? As we were passing this island I asked whether it was inhabited. I understood from the mulatto that there was a house on it. A farm, I fancied, they meant. So I asked them to put me ashore on the beach and keep the boat for their trouble. This, I imagine, was just what they wanted. The rest you know."

After pronouncing these words he lost suddenly all control over himself. He paced to and fro rapidly, till at last he broke into a run; his arms went like a windmill and his ejaculations became very much like raving. The burden of them was that he "denied nothing, nothing!" I could only let him go on, and sat out of his way, repeating, "*Calmez-vous, calmez-vous*," at intervals, till his agitation exhausted itself.

I must confess, too, that I remained there long after he had crawled under his mosquito-net. He had entreated me not to leave him; so, as one sits up with a nervous child, I sat up with him—in the name of humanity—till he fell asleep.

On the whole, my idea is that he was much more of an anarchist than he confessed to me or to himself; and that, the special features of his case apart, he was very much like many other anarchists. Warm heart and weak head—that is the word of the riddle; and it is a fact that the bitterest contradictions and the deadliest conflicts of the world are carried on in every individual breast capable of feeling and passion.

From personal inquiry I can vouch that the story of the convict mutiny was in every particular as stated by him.

When I got back to Horta from Cayenne and saw the "anarchist" again, he did not look well. He was more worn, still more frail, and very livid indeed under the grimy smudges of his calling. Evidently the meat of the company's main herd (in its unconcentrated form) did not agree with him at all.

It was on the pontoon in Horta that we met; and I tried to induce him to leave the launch moored where she was and follow me to Europe there and then. It would have been delightful to think of the excellent manager's surprise and disgust at the poor fellow's escape. But he refused with unconquerable obstinacy.

"Surely you don't mean to live always here!" I cried. He shook his head.

"I shall die here," he said. Then added moodily, "Away from them."

Sometimes I think of him lying open-eyed on his horseman's gear in the low shed full of tools and scraps of iron—the anarchist slave of the Marañon estate, waiting with resignation for that sleep which "fled" from him, as he used to say, in such an unaccountable manner.